SARANORMAL

Spirits
of the
Season

by Phoebe Rivers

SIMON SPOTLIGHT
New York London Toronto Sydney New Delhi

SIMON SPOTLIGHT
An imprint of Simon & Schuster Children's Publishing Division
1230 Avenue of the Americas, New York, New York 10020
Copyright © 2012 by Simon & Schuster, Inc.
All rights reserved, including the right of reproduction in whole or in part in any form.
SIMON SPOTLIGHT and colophon are registered trademarks of Simon & Schuster, Inc.
Text by Heather Alexander
For information about special discounts for bulk purchases, please contact Simon & Schuster Special Sales at 1-866-506-1949 or business@simonandschuster.com.
Manufactured in the United States of America 0812 OFF
First Edition 10 9 8 7 6 5 4 3 2 1
ISBN 978-1-4424-5223-7 (pbk)
ISBN 978-1-4424-5379-1 (hc)
ISBN 978-1-4424-5224-4 (eBook)
Library of Congress Catalog Card Number 2012934012

Prologue

Christmas was over.

Scraps of red-and-gold paper and curls of ribbons littered the floor. Mike Collins surveyed all the crumpled tissue poking out from empty boxes and sighed.

I should've thought to ask Sara to clean up before bed, he thought. *That's what a good father would do.*

He shook his head to clear the doubt.

No, that's what a mother *would do. I am a good father,* he reminded himself.

He'd given Sara everything she'd asked for this Christmas. Clothes. Nail polish. Even a new phone. But all the colorful and sparkly presents never managed to fill the gaping hole in their lives. And, boy, had he tried. He'd spent the last twelve years trying.

SARANORMAL

He was tired. Of trying. Of keeping secrets.

Sara needed things that couldn't be wrapped up and put under the Christmas tree. Things they didn't talk about. But what was there to say? He couldn't bring Natalie, her mother, his wife, his love, back to life. The pain of her death should have softened by now, but whenever he gazed at Sara, the rawness ripped through him. She looked just like her mother.

He shook open a plastic garbage bag in a feeble attempt to return order to their small family room. Family room. He wondered at the name. Did just a father and his twelve-year-old daughter make a family? He used to think so, but Sara was getting older. A teenager soon. He'd kept her so isolated. Had he been wrong?

The doubts again. Clogging his brain.

His eyes drifted to the black side table. He thought of the envelope nestled inside the narrow drawer. It had been sitting there unopened for over a week. When it first appeared in his mailbox, he'd wanted to dump it in the trash. Instead, he'd tucked it in the drawer, convincing himself he was too busy decorating the tree and buying gifts to read it. But that wasn't the truth.

The return address scared him.

Stellamar, New Jersey.

It was from her.

Mike walked over to the table and pulled open the drawer. He took out the envelope and held it up. He inhaled. Would it smell like Natalie did after her morning walks on the Jersey shore? Damp and salty, yet sweet? No. All he could smell was pine from their Christmas tree.

He sank into the gray tweed armchair, the cushion long ago molded to fit his body. Slowly he ripped open the envelope and pulled out a card.

He was finally ready. At least, he hoped so.

The front showed glittery snowflakes against a blue sky. Silver-embossed script proclaimed *Happy Holidays!* A typical store-bought card. But inside the card were three pages covered on both sides in neat, slanted script. Mike's fingers trembled as he unfolded the pages. The message inside would not be typical.

Nothing Lady Azura ever said or did was typical.

Dear Mike,

I have waited so long to write this letter. For years,

I have wanted to reach out to you and to Sara, but the time was not right. Not for you. Not for me. The guilt and the pain were only bearable if I didn't speak of it. But I am getting old, and soon there may not be time left.

I think about our lovely Natalie every day. I also think of dear Sara, her mother taken from her only moments after she entered the world.

As you know, Natalie and I were never close during her childhood. Her mother kept her from me. Natalie's mother—my daughter, Diana—couldn't understand me. She couldn't open her mind to possibilities beyond the accepted. When Diana died when Natalie was just nineteen, Natalie finally turned to me. I can't begin to describe the joy she brought me. I never wanted anything to hurt her, and I never wanted to be the messenger of pain.

But that is exactly what happened.

The vision was so strong, so clear, so frequent that I had no choice but to warn Natalie. I knew you both wanted a large family, but I also knew this was not to be. What I did not know was that Sara was already growing inside her. If I had known she was already pregnant, I would never have told her about my vision. But I didn't know, and so I shared what I saw—that Natalie would die if she tried to give birth. I did not make this up. It was written, it was decreed, it was her fate. I only wanted to warn Natalie.

My warning came too late.

You barely knew me, and I had foretold your greatest nightmare. Please believe me when I tell you, I did everything in my power to be wrong. But I could not change what was meant to be.

Hot tears pricked the corners of his eyes, bringing Mike back to the day Sara was born. The day Natalie died. His grief and anger had mixed into one, and he had lashed out at Natalie's kooky grandmother. The doctors had said no one was to blame, but he'd accused Lady Azura of cursing his beautiful wife with her terrible prophecy. Then he'd taken his newborn daughter and fled to California, cutting off all contact with Natalie's only living relative.

Mike, I have had visions so vivid that I had to share them with you. Natalie has come back to me on several occasions. *Oh, the joy to see her again! She is happy, Mike, with how you are raising her daughter. She watches over both of you. Natalie and I have made our peace. She has forgiven me and wishes we had never argued. I know this is difficult for you to understand, but it is with her blessing that I am contacting you.*

I have also had visions of dear Sara. This child is special. She possesses great powers. Powers I am sure she does not understand. Powers I can help her with because we share them. Mike, I know you did not believe in my powers, but I believe the years may have changed you. As you have raised Sara these past twelve years, can you honestly tell me you have not sensed that your daughter is special? That she is like no other child? I am writing to you on Sara's behalf. Think about her. You know deep down about her, don't you?

The old woman's crazy, he told himself. She'd always believed she could communicate with the dead and see into the future and who knew what else. He and Natalie used to joke about her grandmother's kookiness. He bit his lip at the memory.

Mike's thoughts moved to Sara. To her as a little girl, always talking to imaginary friends. To the girl scared of strange places. The girl who had been plagued by terrible nightmares. The girl whose eyes often focused elsewhere, looking at something unseen.

Could it be? Could she have some sort of paranormal ability?

No, Sara's just shy, he told himself for the millionth time. *A dreamer. Creative.*

But a small part of his brain wondered if that was it, and had wondered about this for some time now.

He turned back to the letter.

I stayed away so long because I thought Natalie would have wanted it that way. I knew you did as well. Now I want nothing more than to meet my great-granddaughter. I have no desire to interfere with your lives, I just long for a connection—a connection that I feel would help Sara. I understand what it's like to see what others do not. From across the country, I can sense Sara's distress and fear. I can make her less afraid.

I still live in the large house by the boardwalk.

There are plenty of rooms. Too many. I would love nothing more than for the two of you to come. Mike, we are family. Please do not wait too long. Sara has many questions, and I have answers. Natalie would have wanted it this way.

He stared at Lady Azura's sure, steady signature for a long time. His mind churned. He'd taken Sara to the other side of the country to escape misery. But emptiness had followed. He thought about his beautiful, fair-haired daughter. She was not like other girls her age. So scared. So anxious.

He shook his head, not wanting to believe Lady Azura's hocus-pocus nonsense about Sara. She was fine. She was just missing a mother. Now he wondered if keeping her from her mother's only living family had been a mistake. He'd never even told Sara that Lady Azura existed.

Suddenly his actions all those years ago seemed foolish. Grief had led him to blame a wacky old woman. Her prophecy had just been a strange coincidence. She hadn't caused Natalie's death.

He slid his cell phone from his pocket.

A number was written below the signature, and he dialed it before he could think better of it.

She answered on the first ring.

It wasn't until July that Mike told Sara. Not about Lady Azura. Not about her mother. Not about the phone call and who the old woman truly was. Just that he'd decided to move them from California to Stellamar, New Jersey. He said it was for work.

He hated lying, but he couldn't risk Sara being hurt. Lady Azura had agreed to the strict rules he'd laid out. She'd promised never to reveal that she was Sara's great-grandmother. She would merely be the woman they were renting from and nothing more until Mike thought Sara was ready to know the truth.

He doubted that day would ever come. But he felt he owed it to Sara to try living in Stellamar, just in case Lady Azura was right, and they were meant to be together.

Chapter 1

I laughed the kind of laughter that takes over your body and makes you feel as if you have to pee.

"Do you dare me to wear this to school?" Lily Randazzo teased. She posed with one hand on her hip, as if she was being photographed for a fashion magazine. But no fashion magazine would feature the ridiculous frilly patchwork apron or the silly knit cap covered with dozens of green and red pom-poms she was wearing.

"You would never," I said, still laughing. "It goes beyond all acceptable ugly."

"That's what makes the combo so great," Lily said, pulling off the hat and apron and placing them back on the store's table. "It's so repulsive that it crosses that line into cool." She eyed them again. "Or not."

"Not," I agreed. I'd already decided to come back later and buy the ugly hat for Lily. She'd laugh on Christmas morning when she opened it. Our inside joke.

I had a best friend and inside jokes. Unbelievable. Everything was so different here in Stellamar.

Better.

"Sara, what am I possibly going to buy here?" Lily whispered. She pulled out a piece of notebook paper scribbled with a list of at least thirty names. "I have to get gifts for all these cousins. Everyone comes to our house on Christmas Eve. A cozy dinner for sixty. Mom started cooking last summer!"

I tucked my long blond hair behind my ears and stared at Lily's list. She had more relatives in and around this tiny town than the town library had books. Or so it seemed. Of course, our town was really small and so was its library, but she still had *a lot*.

"My whole list can fit on a Post-it note," I said. "Dad and Lady Azura. That's it."

But two was more than one, I knew. Way more. Until recently, it would've only been Dad on my list.

I glanced around the store, the Salty Crab, owned

by Lily's aunt Delores. It was a mystery how this woman was related to Lily. Lily had style. She wore cute outfits, oversize sunglasses, and lots of silver jewelry. The Salty Crab sold dresses that could double as tablecloths, sweaters with holiday themes, candles in the shapes of elves and reindeer, and lots of chunky plastic necklaces.

"We could walk somewhere else," I suggested, pointing out the window to Beach Drive.

Lily picked up a snow globe of the Stellamar boardwalk. "My mom says I have to get some stuff here. Family pity. What about you?" She pointed to a nearby display. "Tie with a huge Santa face for your dad?"

"Going to pass on that," I said. "I'm making my gifts. For Dad, I'm decorating a wooden box with some tiny shells I found on the beach."

"You're so good with crafty things," Lily said. "What about Lady Azura?"

"I don't know," I confided. "I want to make her something too, but it has to be special. You know?"

"Totally one-of-a-kind," Lily agreed. "Nobody else is like her."

I watched the tiny snowflakes fall inside the glass

ball as Lily shook it. After months of sharing a house with the old woman, I still didn't know a lot about her. Nothing personal. But I did know we had a connection. We saw things the same way.

A way I couldn't even begin to explain to Lily.

A way no one else could imagine.

"That's it. I'm getting snow globes for all the cousins who work on the boardwalk." Lily grinned. "Half the list is done." She turned to me. "Are you supposed to get Mrs. Martino something?"

"Seriously?" I wrinkled my nose. "I'm not the one dating her, my dad is. Besides, she makes me call her *Janelle*."

"She'll always be Dina's mom," Lily pointed out. "Just the name brings fear to the hearts of middle school girls everywhere!"

"I know. My dad says Janelle's really nice, but I keep thinking if she's the one responsible for releasing Dina into the world, then she can't be all she seems."

"You think she's hatching a diabolical plot?" Lily's dark brown eyes twinkled. Dina Martino was a grade older than we were, but everyone at our school knew her. The mean girls were always known. Supermean

13

girls, like Dina, were legendary.

"No. I just think Janelle's clueless about her daughters. Dad dragged us all out for a family dinner last weekend. Dina's older sister, Chloe, was dressed like they were hosting a beauty pageant at the Chinese restaurant. Sparkly dress and stiletto heels. She and Dina talked about shopping and clothes and hair extensions as if I wasn't even there. The fortune cookie said more to me than they did."

"Did your cookie predict that your dad will keep dating Janelle?" Lily asked.

"It said something weird like 'It is better to be the hammer than the nail.'"

"You should ask Lady Azura." Lily's tone turned serious. "She could look at the tea leaves or the tarot cards."

"I don't need a fortune-teller to tell me this won't last. My dad's dated lots of women. None of them ever work out. He can't get over my mom," I explained. "Janelle has no chance. I'm not worried about her."

"What about Dina?"

"She's decided I don't exist. That's working for me."

"She always trips Miranda in dance class. Her foot

appears out of nowhere, and our teacher never sees it. She just thinks Miranda's gotten really spastic," Lily reported. "Miranda used to stand in the front row. Now she's in the back. Guess who dances in front now?"

"Dina, of course."

Miranda Rich was the most graceful girl I'd ever met. If Dina could pull that off, there was no telling the heights of her meanness.

I zipped up my red down parka to my chin and followed Lily outside. The gray clouds hung low and heavy, but there hadn't been snow yet. December 15. Ten more days. I hoped I'd get my first white Christmas.

Half the stores on Beach Drive were closed. Stellamar was a summer town. No one bought inflatable rafts, painted hermit crabs, or beach umbrellas in December. Lily inspected Seasons Sports Stop's small window display, which was basically a bunch of sports equipment heaped into a gift-wrapped box.

"What are you getting Jayden?" she asked.

"What?"

"*Jayden*," Lily repeated.

"I heard. Wait. You think I should get him something?" My breathing quickened. Total panic. Jayden

Mendes was so cute, with his thick brown hair and warm brown eyes. We talked all the time at school now. Sometimes he texted me. But we were just friends. That was all. I hadn't even considered getting him something.

"Maybe." Lily's voice held that secretive singsong quality.

"What do you know?" I demanded.

She stalled, twirling a strand of her wavy, dark hair around her finger. "He told me not to tell you."

"Lily!"

"Okay, you forced me. Jayden asked me what kind of things you like," she revealed.

"Why?"

"I think he's going to get you a Christmas gift!" Lily beamed. "Isn't that great?"

"No. That's horrible. That means I have to get him something too." My voice squeaked. Until I moved here, I'd practically never even talked to a boy. I'd just started flirting with Jayden a little. Now I had to buy him a gift? "How about a soccer ball?" I pointed to the window display.

"It's kind of lame," Lily replied. "I mean, what if he

gets you something good, like a necklace, and you give him a ball? What does that say?"

I groaned. "What's a gift supposed to say?"

"My cousin Dawn Marie says if a guy gets you jewelry, then he really likes you. My cousin Jessie told me if you get a guy a video game, it says you don't want to hang out with him—"

"Because why?" I wasn't following all this.

"Because you're telling him to go spend time with his video game instead of you!"

"But don't games have two players? We could play together."

Lily shrugged. "You should talk to my cousin Tori. She's always buying gifts for boys. She once bought— Oh, look, there's Adam hanging lights." She pointed to a nearby seafood restaurant. "He's Uncle Lenny's son. I'm going to say hi. Be right back."

I watched Lily scamper down the sidewalk. She never walked. She always skipped or danced. She was always in motion.

What was I going to get Jayden? I wondered. Could I make him something? Or was that too weird? What did I want the gift to say?

I turned back to the sports store window for one last look. Maybe there was something—

I gasped.

A man had appeared.

He stood next to me. Extremely close. So close I could smell him. Musty, almost sour.

I stepped back. "Excuse me," I mumbled.

He wore a khaki uniform with gold buttons, heavy brown boots, and a hard rounded hat. An American flag patch was sewn on one sleeve.

The other sleeve fluttered in the slight breeze.

Empty. The soldier had only one arm.

He leaned toward me, his head inches from mine. Dangerously close. His face was young and extremely pale.

As if all the life had drained from him.

The pungent smell grew stronger. A smell I'd smelled before. The odor of death.

He locked his gray eyes with mine, and in that instant, I knew.

The man was dead.

Chapter 2

I ran.

Away from the man. Away from death. Away from ghosts that were forever following me.

"In here," I said, tugging Lily's scarf, pulling her with me.

"Really?" Lily followed, calling good-bye to Adam.

A bell rang as I pushed through the first door I found. "Welcome to Coastal Decor. Happy holidays!" a petite woman with frizzy red hair greeted us.

"You too," Lily said, not looking at the woman, but staring strangely at me.

I peered out the large front window, scanning the sidewalk. He was gone. Disappeared.

Or hiding.

Waiting.

"Can I help you?" the woman asked.

"I think we're here to buy a sofa for the boy she likes. You know, so she can sit next to him," Lily replied. "Or maybe candlesticks."

I gazed around the small shop, cluttered with wooden tables made from ship's wheels, anchor-printed pillows, blue-and-white nautical-themed sofas and chairs.

"N-no," I stuttered. "That's not it."

"Really? I'm thinking that lamp says Jayden to me." She pointed to a lamp in the shape of a mermaid.

"Are you interested in that?" The woman hurried over.

"No. Sorry. I—uh—thought this was a different store." I checked the sidewalk again. All clear. "Let's go," I told Lily.

"Whatever you say." Lily followed me out of the store. "Though I'm thinking every boy at school wants starfish napkin rings."

"Stop it!" I found myself smiling, even though I still felt queasy.

On the sidewalk, I looked around. Really looked. Not at the beach-town stores that lined the main street. Not at the Salvation Army Santa waving his bell at the corner. Or at the lampposts wrapped with pine garlands and twinkling white lights.

But at all the people.

The dead people.

The ghosts.

I had never seen so many in one place.

Peering out of windows. Sitting on benches. Boarding the bus. Wearing clothing from every decade. Old men. Young women. Children.

Shimmering, vibrating with an intensity that made my head throb.

Everywhere. They were everywhere.

"I need to get back," I told Lily.

I couldn't be here. Not with them.

"Okay, let's go." She turned to walk toward our street. We lived two houses away from each other.

Their energy pulled at me.

"I need to go now. I mean, I'm really late." My voice faltered. "I'm going to run. Okay?"

Lily hesitated. "Sure."

"Talk to you later?"

"Okay."

I began to run. Down Beach Drive onto Ocean Grove Road, not stopping until I reached our huge yellow Victorian with burnt-orange trim on Seagate Drive.

I leaned over, hands on my thighs, panting. As I caught my breath, I wondered at Lily. She never asked questions. Every time I acted weird, she just went with it. Never took it personally. Never made me tell her the truth. The truth I'd kept secret from everyone.

I saw ghosts.

I'd been seeing ghosts since I was a little kid.

They used to just appear. Just show up. That was all.

But ever since I'd moved here, they've been wanting things. Seeking me out. Talking to me.

Scaring me.

I climbed the steps onto the huge wooden porch with the decorative railings. Dad and I rented the top two floors from Lady Azura. She lived and worked as a fortune-teller on the first floor.

I unlocked the front door and paused in the foyer. The house was quiet except for the sound of a man singing.

"Fools rush in . . . ," the rich, deep voice sang.

I followed the sound, pushing through the thick, purple velvet curtains draped over the doorway to my right. The room behind the curtains was dark and empty. A crystal ball sat on a round table covered with a red-and-gold cloth in the center of the room. The faint aroma of cinnamon lingered from the candles that were lit when clients came to call. Shelves along the back wall displayed colorful crystals and gemstones, old books with leather spines, and liquids in glass containers. I noticed a dark liquid in a jar that hadn't been there yesterday.

I resisted the urge to pull back the heavy front draperies and let daylight in so I could explore. I loved Lady Azura's fortune-telling room, but I wasn't allowed to go poking around. She was strict about that, and I respected that.

A doorway in the back corner of the room was hidden by another curtain. The man's voice rose from behind it. Some guy from long ago. Lady Azura had a retro record player, and she played his records all the time. At over eighty years old, she wasn't the iPod type.

I didn't know what type she was. I'd never met anyone like her.

"Straight or crooked?" she called. "Take a look."

She always knew when I was outside a room.

I stepped through the curtain, and she turned to me. Her head seemed unnaturally tiny today, poking out from a scarlet sweater with an enormous cowl-neck. With bone-thin arms and legs, Lady Azura seemed small and frail at first glance, but she was the opposite. Her deep brown eyes rimmed with jet-black false eyelashes and thick eyeliner betrayed her fierceness.

"The calendar," she said in her husky voice, when I didn't answer.

I gazed over her shoulder at a worn Advent calendar taped to the wall by her vanity. It was the paper kind in the shape of a bright green Christmas tree, with little windows that opened for the twenty-five days in December leading up to Christmas.

"Straight," I said. The calendar looked out of place in her sleek black-and-white bedroom. Or maybe it was her ultramodern bedroom with its black-lacquered vanity, glass tables, black armless chairs, and stark all-white bedding that was out of place in the run-down old house.

I took a step closer. "Why did you do that?" I asked, pointing to the windows for December 23, 24, and 25. Each window had been taped shut with a small piece of silver duct tape.

"I did that many, many years ago." She sat on the stool by her vanity and scrutinized her face in the brightly lit mirror.

"But why?"

"Some days are diamonds. Some are stones." She opened a silver tube and twisted up a column of dark red lipstick.

"So you don't like Christmas?"

"Of course I like Christmas. Why wouldn't I?" She stared at her reflection as she carefully lined her thin, wrinkled lips.

"Then why stop counting the days after the twenty-second?"

"I am not counting the days. I'm finding the days that count."

I often felt as if she was speaking in code, and I lost my copy of the codebook.

I watched her apply a final coat of lipstick and was struck again by how little I knew about her. True, for a while after Dad moved us in here, I did everything I could to avoid her. But that had changed.

"Do you go anywhere for Christmas?" I asked.

"Where would I go?"

"I don't know. Relatives, maybe. The Randazzos have, like, a billion cousins at their house. When we lived in California, we sometimes went to my aunt Charlotte's house when I was little. That's my dad's sister. She's all organic and vegan, and she'd serve this turkey, but it wasn't really turkey, it was tofu, so Dad and I stopped going."

Lady Azura stood, wobbling slightly on her gold heels. "I'm not fond of turkey, but a good honey ham . . ." She headed through the curtain. "Your dad's out. Something about going to the office, even though it's Saturday. We should have time before he gets home."

I followed her into her fortune-telling room. She'd been helping me since Halloween, since I realized that she could also see the dead. She wasn't scared like me. She'd learned how to control and work her power. That's what she called it. Our power. She was showing me that it was a good thing, not something to fear.

I still wasn't totally convinced.

She turned on two small, fringed lamps, bathing the cozy room with a soft glow. We sat around the table.

"Take a deep breath, Sara." She rested one of her hands on mine. "Your positive energy will bring their positive energy. They are looking for openness. Your fear frustrates them."

"Sometimes they frustrate me," I mumbled.

"You need to protect yourself. The same way a firefighter wears special clothes or you wear sunscreen when you go to sit in the sun. Surround yourself with White Light."

"What's that?"

"It's a feeling of happiness, of calmness, of self-assuredness that comes from within. Bring it up and cover yourself in it, much the same way the Good Witch in *The Wizard of Oz* covered herself in a floating bubble of goodness. Close your eyes and try."

I thought of Glinda the Good Witch. I thought of myself in a bubble. With a wand. And a pouffy dress. I started to giggle. "You came to me, Sara. You asked for my help," Lady Azura reminded me.

"I know. I'm sorry."

"This White Light or bubble will allow you to live your life as you want to live it. It will give you the power to keep the dead at a distance."

I thought about the dead soldier. How he'd brought his face so close to mine. No barriers.

"What was happening today?" I asked. "There were all these spirits in town. Usually there are one or two, here and there. But this was strange."

"It's Christmastime," Lady Azura said simply. "The Twelve Days."

"Like the song?" I asked.

"Not quite. There is a . . . let's call it a window, that's open for the twelve days before the holiday. During this time, the departed return to visit or check up on loved ones. It's not only those who are trapped here, trying to resolve issues, but all who miss someone dear."

"And now's the time?"

"The Twelve Days started yesterday, on the fourteenth, and end on the twenty-fifth. I should have warned you."

"Do other people, people not like us, know they're here?"

"To many people, the holidays are bittersweet, for they can feel the tug and the presence of those whom they've lost, but they don't know how to describe or process it. It is more of a lingering feeling than a realization."

I thought back on all the Christmases in our little stucco house in California. The tree in the family room and the ornament I made in preschool with a photo of Mom on it.

"Do you think my mom comes back?" I asked quietly.

Lady Azura grasped both my hands in her cold, bony ones. "I do not know, my child. I would like to think so."

"If I see all the others, then wouldn't it make sense that I would see her, too?" I'd struggled with this question for years, turning it over and over in my head. Why couldn't I see the one dead person who meant anything to me? Where was she?

"Nothing is ever that simple," she said. "Maybe in time."

"I don't want to wait!" I pulled my hands away from her. "I don't want to keep seeing some creepy guy. I never got to see my mom when she was alive. Don't you at least think I should get to see her now?"

"There are many people I would like to see too." She stared down at her hands. "I miss my love."

She said it so quietly, I almost didn't hear. Suddenly I realized how alone Lady Azura was. As far as I knew, she had no relatives. Or at least none that ever visited or called.

"Where is your family?" I asked.

"Gone." She shifted in her large armchair. "My husband, Richard, died more than twenty years ago."

"I'm sorry." I tried to imagine her husband. A dashing businessman, probably. "What was he like?"

"He was an ornithology professor. You know what that is? Birds. He studied birds. Richard traveled all over the world, studying the migratory paths of birds. And when he wasn't traveling, he'd be wading waist deep in the Pine Barrens swamp in search of one feathered friend or another. He was a wonderful man, and a good father, but way too crazy about his birds—"

"Where are your kids?" I interrupted. I didn't mean to ask so bluntly, but the words just came out. Lady

Azura had mentioned a daughter to me, but I didn't know anything about her.

For the first time ever, Lady Azura became flustered. She gazed up at the ceiling for the longest time, and I wondered whether she was angry or if she would cry. Finally she murmured, "I had one child only. A daughter, Diana. I don't anymore."

I didn't know what to say. Did that mean she died? Was it okay for me to ask?

"I'm going to make a cup of tea," she said abruptly. "We'll work on barriers another time. Why don't you go upstairs?"

"Sure," I replied slowly, watching her leave.

Upstairs in my bedroom, I gently closed the door. We lived on the second floor, but technically the third floor was ours too. I had a cool crafts room up there that my dad had made for me, complete with a photo printer and other art supplies. With these two floors all to ourselves, there was way too much space for just the two of us.

As I sat on my bed, I wondered about what had happened to Lady Azura's family. *She must be lonely,* I thought. I couldn't imagine how empty this huge house must have felt to her before Dad and I moved in.

I stared at the framed photos I'd arranged on the wall. Photographs my mom had taken. My favorite one was a picture: a pretty porcelain angel with a halo of blond curls.

Even though I didn't have my mom or many relatives, I had Dad. He always made every holiday fun, especially Christmas. He'd dress as Santa and leave muddy reindeer footprints in our yard. We'd always cook a big dinner together with lots of mashed potatoes.

Suddenly I knew what to do. We'd have a real family Christmas this year. A tree, presents, Santa, even a honey-baked ham—and we'd surprise Lady Azura with it. We'd make her part of our family.

I couldn't wait to tell Dad.

Chapter 3

"Please, stop," I whispered. "Please."

Her wretched sobs continued.

I wrapped my pillow over my head to muffle the sound. I still heard her labored breaths, the sorrow surfacing in strange gasps.

Her crying had been a constant in my life since we'd moved into this house. All day. All night. I'd pretty much learned to ignore it. Block out her pain like bad dentist-office music. But this Sunday morning it had gotten worse. Louder.

There was no chance I was going back to sleep. All the woman in the room next to me did was cry and rock in her rocking chair. All the time. Forever.

An unhappy spirit whom only I could see.

Lady Azura was too old to climb the steep, narrow

staircase. She hadn't been upstairs in years and never saw the spirits that haunted the upper floors. But I'm sure she could hear her today.

Why was the woman so sad? I wondered.

Had she lost her husband? A child? A parent?

What could cause someone such eternal grief?

I hoped that whoever it was knew about the Twelve Days and came back. I wanted the woman to be happy.

I also wanted her to be quiet.

I heard a creak. Then another.

Everything in this old house creaked. The floors. The spirits.

I peeked out from under my pillow, afraid of who I'd see.

"Good, you're up too!" Dad greeted me from my doorway. His brown curls were matted on one side from his pillow, but he wore a wide grin. "Getting in the Christmas spirit? Remember how you could never sleep the night before Christmas?"

"That's over a week away," I grumbled. "It's too early to be that happy."

"What you need is waffles," he proclaimed. "Waffles make everyone happy, especially when the syrup pools in the little squares. Meet you in the kitchen!"

I contemplated staying in bed with my head buried under the pillow. Then I thought about the waffles. Dad was right. Homemade waffles were way better than listening to a spirit cry.

I mixed the batter while Dad greased the waffle iron. Through the window, the first glimmer of morning light cut through the darkness. We spoke in whispers so as not to wake Lady Azura. Not that that was really an issue, since she slept until noon most days. She stayed up way into the night. Sometimes I heard her roaming about, talking to herself.

I filled Dad in on my Christmas surprise.

"Excellent! We need a tree, pronto!" he exclaimed, no longer whispering. "There's a guy selling big ones down by the lighthouse. We'll go today and dig out the box of ornaments and buy some lights and garlands. Maybe a wreath or two."

"If we get a tree today, there's still plenty of time to decorate." I handed him the batter.

"Actually, not really." He gave me a sheepish glance. "I was going to talk to you about that. I'm going away next weekend."

"Where are we going?" I asked, hoisting myself up to sit on the counter.

"Not we, kiddo. Me." He paused. "And Janelle. Ben Lewis, who we work with, is getting married in Philadelphia. We thought we'd go to the wedding and stay over in Philly."

I didn't say anything.

"I thought you could spend the night with Lady Azura. You could invite Lily or some other girls. Have a sleepover. That would be fun, no?"

I still didn't say anything. Dad looked so worried. I knew he was scared that I'd be unhappy spending the night with Lady Azura. But I didn't mind about that. I'd actually wanted to spend time with her, so I could ask her more questions about our powers. I wasn't speaking because I couldn't believe that he actually liked Janelle enough to go away with her.

"So this thing with you and Janelle, is it a real thing?" I asked.

"I don't know what that means, but yes, I like Janelle. A lot."

"What do you like about her?" I hoped that didn't sound too rude . . . but I kind of had to know.

"Janelle's smart. She's funny. We have a good time." He turned to flip the waffle, then turned back to me. "Sara, your mom will always be my first love."

"I know." And I did. I wanted him to be happy and find someone to love. "I just don't think you two are right for each other."

"Because why?"

"Because her daughters are horrible."

"They are not," he protested. "Chloe and Dina are both very sweet. Nice girls."

"And you know this because you met them once in a Chinese restaurant?"

"I've met Chloe and Dina twice, actually. I think they're great."

I couldn't believe Janelle and her daughters had conned my dad. I clamped my lips together to stop myself from telling him that considering I went to school with her mean daughter every day and had a front-row seat for her evil, I had a much better sense of how *not-great* she was.

"You need to spend more time with them," Dad continued. "I bet you have more in common than you realize."

"I don't think—"

"Something is burning!" Lady Azura called from the doorway.

We all turned as a tendril of smoke escaped the waffle iron. Dad grabbed a dish towel and opened the lid, releasing the remains of charred waffle. Lady Azura wrapped her white silk robe tighter around her tiny body as I pushed open the small window by the sink, letting in the icy morning air. Her long hair was wrapped in a matching white silk turban, and without her makeup, her pale, papery skin blended in with the turban.

"What is going on here at this ridiculous hour?" she demanded. Her eyes darted nervously about the room, as if searching for something other than the obvious.

"We're cooking waffles," I explained.

"Burning them, you mean."

"That was just the practice one," Dad explained, greasing the waffle iron again. "Sara distracted me. I'm sorry if we woke you."

Lady Azura sighed and sat at the table. "You didn't. I've been up."

"Why?" I joined her at the table.

Her eyes darted around the room once more. "I can't sleep this time of year."

"I agree," Dad called from the stove. "So much to do."

"So many to wait for," Lady Azura murmured under her breath.

She must be waiting for her husband and her daughter to come back, I realized. What were they like? When I tried to picture her husband, Richard, I kept seeing a man in a dark business suit with the head of a bald eagle.

I watched Lady Azura closely, but she was absorbed in her own distant thoughts. A gem on a gold chain shimmered around her neck as she loosened her grip on her robe.

"That's pretty," I said. The white-green stone glinted in the kitchen's overhead light, causing flashes of pink and blue to intermingle with the green.

She rested one finger on the iridescent stone "Opal," she said.

"What's it for?" Her gemstones were more than just pretty. They had powers, too. She'd already given me some small ones—an aquamarine for courage, a ruby crystal for love, and hematite for protection—and I wore them together on a necklace.

"Opals make wishes come true." Her eyes focused once more on the window.

"Does it work?"

"It's new, but I sincerely hope so."

"What are you wishing for?"

"Ahh, there are many things in your heart that must remain in your heart lest they get spoiled."

I guessed that meant she wasn't going to tell me.

I wanted to know more about the opal, but Dad jumped in. He told Lady Azura about his Philly plans.

"So you want to leave me here, alone with Sara? Two days. Just the two of us?" She didn't sound happy.

"If it's not too much trouble." Dad sounded as surprised as I felt. "She'll be good—"

"Of course she'll be good," Lady Azura snapped. "We both know what the problem is. Mike, it's the week before Christmas. You promised it wouldn't go on this long."

"It won't. Soon. Not now." Dad seemed nervous. Panicked. What was going on?

"I don't want to be in this situation anymore." She

shot him a warning look. A look I couldn't understand. Was I the situation? Did she not want to hang out with me? Was I asking too many questions?

I'd thought Lady Azura and I were getting close. Bonding.

I guess I was wrong.

Chapter 4

"I think she hates me," I confided to Lily as we walked to school the next morning.

"Oh, please, she so doesn't hate you." Lily leaped forward, practicing a dance move she called a grand jeté. "I bet she was talking about your dad dating Dina's mom. She probably looked in her crystal ball and realized what we already know, that it's a huge mistake. That's the situation that's going on too long."

"Maybe." Was that it? I didn't think so. "But she's been kind of cold to me the last couple of days. Like she can't bear to be alone with me. Weird, right?"

"You're definitely weird." Lily pirouetted on the sidewalk in front of Elber's Convenience Store.

"You, the dancing queen, are calling me weird?" I laughed and raised my camera to shoot Lily twirling in front of the green-and-white-striped awning. Ever since I'd been made staff photographer of the *Stellamar Wire*, our school's online newspaper, I'd been taking my camera everywhere.

"How are you going to turn that photo into news?" Lily asked. "Mrs. Notkin likes facts, facts, facts."

"I'll just keep it for myself. There's great motion in it."

"You know, you could always sleep over my house Saturday night when your dad is gone," Lily offered. "My mom loves you."

"Thanks." Lily's mom was great. She treated me like one of her kids. "Maybe I will."

"We need to work on the article on the new donation to the media center. You should take a photo of Mrs. Krell when I interview her. . . ."

I stopped listening.

He was back.

The army guy with the missing arm.

He stood stiffly, as if at attention, alongside old Mr. Rathgeb, the crossing guard by the school. Other kids streamed by, but he remained motionless. Waiting.

Waiting for me.

His face looked drawn, and a weariness clouded his eyes. The fabric of his empty sleeve fluttered in the wind. Then he caught sight of me.

"Of course, a photo of a bunch of new equipment is beyond boring, but if you . . . ," Lily continued as Mr. Rathgeb stopped traffic and waved us into the crosswalk.

The soldier marched forward. Right at me. As if zeroing in on a target.

I glanced behind me at the curb. Should I go back? But then how would I get into the school?

The first warning bell sounded. Kids pushed across the street.

"I need help." His voice was low. He stood in front of me.

I moved to the left, trying to dodge him.

He followed.

I shifted back to the right. He shadowed my every move.

"I need help," he said again.

Centimeters now separated us, and the sour smell of death struck me. I started to gag.

"Sara?" Lily called, suddenly realizing that I'd

stopped in the middle of the street.

She didn't know a dead soldier blocked my path. No one knew.

"Miss?" Mr. Rathgeb stepped toward me. A few other kids turned, curious.

The soldier was much bigger than I was.

A car honked its horn.

I felt everyone staring, waiting.

Then I did it. I faked to the right, then sprang forward with one of Lily's dance leaps, past the soldier. I grabbed Lily's hand, and we ran toward the school.

"Was that supposed to be a grand jeté?" Lily called as we took the front steps two at a time.

"Like it?"

"Inspired." Lily laughed, but her laughter was drowned out by a voice only I could hear. A voice that pleaded, "I need help."

I felt bad, but it was unfair of him. What could I possibly do in the middle of the street in front of all the kids at school?

I heard his voice all through first-period science. A nagging whisper in my head. *I need help, I need help.*

He wasn't here in the classroom. I knew he wasn't. I had to ignore the voice. Block it out.

"Hey." Jayden wandered over to my lab table. We weren't partners today.

"Hey." I wondered how to ask him if he was really getting me a Christmas present. I didn't want to get him something unless I knew for sure he was getting me something. "Only a few more days left."

"Yeah. The days before break last the longest." He held a beaker in his hand. He'd been on his way to the sink to fill it.

"Do you do a big family Christmas?" I asked. I didn't know how to bring it up. I couldn't just come right out and say it. Or could I?

"Kind of. I mean, most of our family is in Atlanta. We're flying down there on the twenty-third." He shifted his weight from foot to foot.

"So when do you get gifts?" I got the word *gifts* in! That was a start.

He shrugged. "Probably in Atlanta. Are you home then? Right before Christmas?"

"Yeah, sure, why?"

"Jayden Mendes, stop talking and start working!"

Miss Klingert called from the front of the room. "What did I say?"

"Start working," Jayden called back. Miss Klingert ran her class like a cheerleading squad.

"Go, go, go!" she called. I could tell she missed her pom-pom days.

Why did he want to know where I'd be right before Christmas? Was he planning on coming over with a present? Now I had two voices battling for space in my head. The dead soldier who wanted help, and me, asking myself baffling questions.

The noise wouldn't stop all day.

I was happy when the final bell rang. I opened my locker door and began to sort through the binders I needed to bring home. Suddenly I felt someone behind me. Watching me. Waiting.

I didn't want to do this in school.

I couldn't speak to him here.

Taking a deep breath, I turned.

Dina Martino cracked her gum and eyed me. She wore a black-and-white-striped blazer over a stretchy black miniskirt. The lacy pink tank under the blazer matched the glossy color on her lips. "I'm here to give you a message. You're supposed to meet us after school tomorrow in the front."

"What?"

"You think I'm happy about this? My mom promised me a new phone case if I came with you guys. I'm only going for that. And if I smile while we're there, it's only for my mom's sake, because believe me, we are never going to be friends."

"Going where?"

"To the mall." Dina rolled her eyes.

"We're going to the mall? Together?"

"Are you stupid?" Dina placed her hands on her hips, as if waiting for an answer. "This was your dad's idea. Spending time together. My mom jumped all over it. 'Girl bonding,' she calls it. So now Mom, Chloe, and I have to drag you to the mall with us tomorrow."

A lot of responses ran through my mind, but I knew if I tried even one of them and it got back to Dad, I'd be in major trouble.

"Sounds like fun." My tone was far from fun, but it didn't matter. Dina had already left, not caring what I thought.

How could Dad do this to me? I wondered, as I

walked home by myself. I was glad Lily had stayed after for extra help in math. I needed to fix this with Dad, to make it not happen, before she ever heard about it. She would find it too funny.

"I need help."

The voice was back. Not in my head. In front of me. The army guy was standing on the sidewalk.

He pulled his hat from his head with his one good hand and held it against his chest. "Take me to my betrothed, please."

I darted around him and kept walking.

"I need help." His footsteps were silent, yet I knew he was following me. "Please take me to my betrothed."

I didn't know what a betrothed was. I didn't know where he wanted me to take him. I quickened my pace, but he moved closer, practically becoming my shadow.

I was afraid to stop and talk to him. He was too close. His energy pulled at me, scrambled my thoughts, and made it hard to breathe.

"She's waiting for me," he whispered into my ear.

My legs took off before I could think. Running.

Running as fast as I could down the sidewalks toward home. My rubber soles slapped the pavement, and the crisp air burned my lungs, but I kept going. I had to.

I was trying to outrun a ghost.

Was that even possible?

Was he still behind me?

I turned to look.

Chapter 5

Gone. He was gone.

I slowed when I reached Seagate Drive. There were others lurking. On the wide Victorian porch of the pink house at the corner. In the branches of the old oak tree in front of the Fergusons'. But they didn't want anything from me. They were here to see loved ones, not me.

Spirits haunted our porch too. An old woman on the double swing, forever knitting. A man in a cap running his fingers over the brown, shriveled leaves in the planter, searching for life. A pale face at the bay window, eyes darting about.

I waved to Lady Azura, the pale face very much alive. What was she looking for? I realized then that no one had come.

The spirit window had been open for four days already.

"They'll be here," I told her when she met me in the foyer.

"Who?" She wore a long green silk dress cinched at the waist with a thin belt.

"Your family. I know you're probably lonely with no family around."

"I *do* have family." She sounded angry.

"I didn't mean it like that," I fumbled. "I mean, you said you miss your love. Your husband will come this week, you'll see."

"I loved Richard, but I love others as well."

"And they all died?"

"Not all."

"Do you have a boyfriend?" Maybe one of her fortune-telling clients was more than a client! Maybe he was someone special.

"No." She gave a short laugh. "My boyfriend days are over." She sighed. "I've had my true love. Now I'm left missing him. Missing all the time we could've had together. Our paths seem so clear. Then destiny changes the route, yet our hearts yearn to move forward along the same road." Lady Azura trained her gaze on me. "You and I, we are forever searching for what was taken from us."

I didn't know what we were talking about. Her husband? My mother? Something else entirely? "I don't understand."

"I am trying, Sara. Believe me, my child, I am trying."

"Trying what?"

"To get you the answers you need." She closed her eyes as if pained. Then she reached into her pocket and pulled out a small iridescent gemstone. She held it out to me. "An opal for your necklace. So your wishes come true."

"What wishes?" I asked, taking the shiny stone. There was a tiny hole in it to add it to my necklace.

"The small ones and the big one." She turned and disappeared behind the purple curtain, before I could say thank you.

"I am not going," I repeated that night.

"You've told me five times already." Dad stood on a stepladder, attempting to straighten the tinsel on our tree. We had placed the tree in the front sitting room, so Lady Azura could enjoy it too. I'd noticed that the division between her part of the house and ours had started to blur. Dad and I were spending a lot more time on the first floor.

"But you're not listening to me." I was so frustrated I wanted to scream. Dad refused to let me out of this mall disaster. I had tried every argument.

"Look, kiddo." He climbed down and placed his hand on my shoulder. "Do this as a favor for me. Please."

What could I do? I saw how much this silly outing meant to him. He rarely asked me for anything. It was always him doing stuff for me. "Fine," I agreed. "I'll go. For you."

"Thank you." His face brightened. He pulled out his wallet and handed me two twenties. "Spend it on holiday gifts. Or decorations."

"You owe her more," Lady Azura piped up from a side chair, where she flipped through this week's *People* magazine.

"Sara and I are good," Dad replied. "Nobody owes anybody anything."

Lady Azura grunted. "That's not how I see it."

"It's okay," I assured her. "I'll suffer through it."

"I'm not worried about that. He owes you more than that."

"Not now." Dad cut her off.

"When?" she asked. "You've been here five months."

"I need more time." Dad shot her a pleading look. "I think we should discuss this later."

"Later when? Seven months? Ten months? A year?" she countered.

"What are you guys talking about?" I asked.

They both ignored me.

"Soon," Dad promised. "Just give me more time to figure things out and make a plan."

"You've been here too long, Mike." Lady Azura stood and headed toward her rooms. "I can't bear it any longer."

"Wait!" Dad raced after her, their voices becoming muffled as they disappeared into her fortune-telling room.

I waited, baffled, beneath the half-decorated tree. The tree meant for the first Christmas the three of us were to share together. But now it sounded like Lady Azura wanted us out of the house. Lady Azura had been grumpy for the past few days. I thought it was because her dead husband was a no-show. That she was missing her true love.

Now I wasn't so sure. Had something bad happened between her and my dad?

Chapter 6

"The best! The absolute best!" Janelle cried. She held the sweater up for me to see. Pale pink fluffy angora with crystal heart-shaped buttons and pink fake fur around the color. "It's *so* you."

If I'd been dipped in a cotton-candy machine, I thought.

"Wool makes me itch," I said lamely.

This shopping trip was making me itch.

"Oh, I hear you, girlfriend." Janelle replaced the sweater and rifled through a nearby rack of sparkly spandex tanks. "Scratchy fabrics are out. I always tell Chloe and Dina to treat their skin right. Softness is key."

"That's why I always exfoliate and moisturize," Chloe said. She looked exactly like her mom. Same long dark hair; same cat's-eye glasses, except hers had rhinestones; same lilac-y smell. "I'm sixteen now, but I started when I was your age. You should too." She peered at my face. "You actually have great skin. I'm really into makeup and skin."

"Thanks," I yelled over the pop music blaring from the store's speakers. A girl sang a chorus of *"Honey, honey, honey,"* accompanied by a reverberating techno beat.

"Don't you love Pink Sunrise?" Janelle asked. "It's Dina's favorite store."

"I've actually never been here."

"Obviously," Dina muttered. She stood alongside her older sister, flipping through a display of pink earmuffs. Everything in the store was some shade of pink. The walls, the clothes, even the hangers.

Doesn't Janelle realize Dad doesn't do stores like this? I thought. He was a fan of catalogs. He'd drop one on my bed and I'd fold down some pages and the clothes would arrive in a brown box at our door without musical accompaniment. Sometimes, in California, my aunt Charlotte took me shopping. But Aunt Charlotte only wore clothes made from natural fibers, like hemp, and without artificial dyes. Neon pink spandex was not part of her vocabulary.

"Are you having fun?" Janelle asked eagerly. She really seemed to care. "I thought you'd enjoy a girly-girl day out."

"It's great," I lied with a forced smile. It might have actually been okay, maybe even fun, if I'd gone with Lily. There were some things in the store I liked, but all of it together, combined with Dina, was overwhelming.

"This would look fantastic on you." She pulled out a one-sleeved tunic top with magenta stripes and a pair of silver stretchy leggings. "You've got to lose the sweatshirts and jeans and discover your California-glam look. You're so pretty, Sara! If we just spruce up your wardrobe a teeny bit, you would be a total knockout!"

"I agree." Chloe stood alongside her mother, looking me up and down. "She needs a whole new look."

"Makeover!" Janelle cried, reaching for three more pink outfits. "Dina, help me. Grab me some clothes for Sara."

"On it." I saw the glint in Dina's eye. There was no way I was trying on anything she picked.

Thirteen tops, four skinny jeans, three leggings, a miniskirt, and forty-five minutes in the cramped dressing room later, Janelle had assembled an outfit that she declared was "out of this world."

"You are orbiting another planet in that, Sara!" she told me enthusiastically.

I sort of liked it, actually— pale pink skinny jeans with a soft white tunic-style top that had a sprinkle of shimmer—until Dina came up behind me, scowling. "Alien. Another planet is right," she whispered.

Janelle insisted on buying the entire outfit for me, saying it was an early Christmas present. There was no way I could ever wear it to school, though. Dina would have everyone laughing at me. I followed Janelle out of the store and into the mall.

People were everywhere.

Pushing. Shopping. Talking. Waiting. Watching.

I froze.

"What's wrong?" Janelle asked, turning back. Dina kept walking.

"It's just so crowded," I murmured, trying to clear my suddenly spinning head.

There were so many here. Groups of them.

"Christmas brings the crowds," Janelle explained. "Everyone loves to shop."

Even the dead? Spirits were all over. The weight of their presence sucked the air out like a vacuum. My body stiffened and my lungs tightened. The ghosts pushed at me, giving me no room to even stand.

White Light. I remembered Lady Azura's White Light. I tried to think happy thoughts. If I relaxed, they'd back off. Happy thoughts.

"Ew, what is wrong with her?" Dina's voice suddenly rang out. "Why does she look like that? I'm telling you, Mom, call her dad and have him get her. Normal people's skin does not look that green."

"Are you okay?" Janelle asked me, worried.

"Fine," I croaked as I searched for an escape. Anywhere. Happy thoughts had no chance with Dina around. "How about we go there?" I pointed to a small makeup boutique that looked fairly empty.

"We can try on makeup!" Chloe squealed. She grabbed my hand and hurried me over to a counter.

"Maybe they have something for her gross green skin tone," Dina said, just loud enough for me to hear and her mom to miss.

I wanted to say something nasty back, but I knew it wouldn't work. Dina could easily out-nasty me without even trying. My fingers fumbled at the neckline of my white sweatshirt and found my necklace. I knew the feel of each crystal. I reached for the smooth opal.

I wish she'd stop being so mean to me, I thought.

Dina didn't say anything else. Had it worked? Or was she saving it for later, when her mom couldn't hear?

Dina dragged her mom away to sample nail polish, while Chloe brushed shades of blush on the inside of my wrist and chattered on about the right colors for me. I let her. I was happy to be away from all those spirits.

Their neediness. Their noise.

I gazed about. A few other customers sampled the makeup. All were living, except one. An older man in a pin-striped suit and jaunty red bow tie. He seemed out of place, even for a ghost.

I watched as he silently followed an older woman through the aisles. She had a helmet of teased white hair and wore a simple navy dress and matching handbag. Every time she stopped, he stopped, as if they were truly shopping together. But they weren't. She didn't know he was there.

Then she stopped and opened her handbag to pull out a tissue. With a flick of his invisible wrist, he slyly knocked a bottle of perfume into her open bag. No one saw. Not the salesladies. Not the old woman, who closed her bag without looking down.

The woman headed past me. So did the spirit.

I couldn't believe it. The ghost had just shoplifted!

"It's her favorite," he said in a scratchy voice.

I turned to stare at him.

"Sara, stop moving. We need the bright light to see what colors work." Chloe tried to move my face back.

I kept staring at him. Through him.

"I've given my wife a bottle every Christmas since we fell in love in high school," the man confided, his voice echoing strangely. "I still do." He smiled at me, then followed her into the mall.

Should I tell someone? I wondered.

Tell them what? I would only get the old woman in trouble. I didn't want to do that. She didn't mean to steal.

True love lived on, I realized, thinking about the old couple. It didn't go away.

I couldn't stop wondering about it, marveling at it, as Janelle led us to the food court for frozen yogurt. Maybe the concept of love living beyond the grave was my White Light, because all the spirits seemed to back off and leave me alone while I thought about it. At least until Dina and I stood side by side at the toppings bar.

"Healthy much?" Dina raised her eyebrows, as I scooped heaping portions of M&M's and crushed Oreos into my paper cup.

"Maybe you should try some sweetness," I countered.

"Ohhh! The alien has a comeback!" She pulled out her phone and began texting rapidly. What was she saying about me to her friends?

So much for the power of the opal, I thought. I reached over Dina and her phone for the gummy bear ladle, started scooping . . . and he appeared.

Squeezed right between me and Dina.

The army guy. Paler and more upset than before. The stench of death turned my stomach.

"Please lead me to her." He grasped my outstretched

arm with his one good hand. An icy sensation ricocheted toward my elbow.

I tried to push him away. He wouldn't leave and he wouldn't let go. I held a spoonful of gummy bears frozen in midair.

"Please," he repeated.

"No!" I whispered. "Why won't you leave me alone?"

"You live with my love. You live in her house!"

"I can't talk to you now," I hissed. "Later. When we're alone."

He brought his face even closer. His gray eyes were so clear it was as if they were windows, and I could see deep into him. I saw his longing, his misery, how lost he was.

His emotions swirled inside me. His sadness became my sadness.

"She misses me terribly." His icy grip on me tightened. "You must know that she is missing me."

"You're him!" I cried. I flung my hand in the air, loosening his grip and sending the spoonful of gummy bears flying.

"Hey!" Dina screamed, as the candies pelted her in the face.

Suddenly it all made sense to me. This must be the guy the spirit in the rocking chair cried about all the time. Her missing love.

"She cries for you," I whispered, digging the spoon back into the bucket of gummy bears.

"Take me back to her. Please?" the army guy pleaded.

"You want *me* to take *you*?" I asked.

"Seriously?" Dina burst out laughing. "You are seriously talking to the gummy bears. O-M-G! Priceless!"

I spiraled back to reality. Dina was videotaping me with her phone.

What was I doing? What was I saying? I was talking to candy! I must look crazy.

"I got it at all." Dina grinned, holding up the screen for me to see. "You're actually telling the little gummy guy you'll talk to him later when you're alone!"

"Give me that!" I yelled, reaching for Dina's phone.

"As if." Dina grabbed my sleeve. "We're going to the bathroom, Mom," she called to Janelle. She dragged me across the food court into a ladies' room that was littered with wet toilet paper.

"I'm going to post this on every website

imaginable," Dina announced triumphantly. "Every kid at school will see this and know what a total freak you are!"

I cringed. I'd worked so hard to be normal here. Not a girl who talked to ghosts. Or gummy bears. With one click, she would ruin it all.

I couldn't let that happen. "What do you want to delete it?"

"Simple." Dina checked the stalls to make sure we were alone, then turned to me. "Help me break up my mom and your dad."

Chapter 7

I was expecting some horrible, humiliating deed. I was not expecting Dina to suggest something I'd been up all night thinking myself.

I stared at her. She stared back, one hand on her hip, the other grasping her phone. What was she up to? I wondered.

"Why don't you like my dad?"

"Are you going to help me or am I posting this video?"

"You didn't answer my question."

"I don't have to." She thrust the phone toward me. "I have the video. In or out?"

I wasn't sure how I felt. I didn't think Janelle and my dad were a good match, but Dad was happy, and Janelle seemed to really like my dad. It wasn't right for me to mess with that. Then again, if I didn't help Dina, I'd be stuck spending even more time with her. Not to mention the issue of the video. I had no choice.

"In," I said. "What do you want me to do?"

Dina bit her glossed lip. For the first time, she seemed unsure. "I'm still perfecting my plan. I'll get back to you."

She had no plan, I realized.

"Let's go. My mom's going to miss us." Dina tucked her phone in the pocket of her black jeans.

"What about the video?" I demanded. "You need to delete it."

"Not so fast. Not until they're broken up. But don't worry, you have my word." She noticed my raised eyebrows. "Trust me, Sara. We're friends now."

All at once, I wondered about that wish I'd made on the opal earlier. This wasn't how I'd thought it would turn out.

Dad was asleep. The house was quiet. Except for the crying.

I tiptoed down the darkened hall, careful to avoid all the squeaky floorboards.

I stopped outside her room. The pink room with the high ceilings. The Room of Sadness.

I twisted the glass doorknob and entered slowly. Her chair faced a window and doors leading to a balcony overlooking the bay. The light of the moon shimmered through the glass, making her long white nightgown glow. The young woman didn't stop rocking or weeping. I didn't know if she knew I stood beside her.

"Um . . . hi," I started. I'd never talked to a spirit without him or her talking to me first. I wasn't sure how to begin. "I'm Sara."

I waited. She held her thin hands to her face, unable to control her sobs.

"I know you're sad. I mean, I can hear you crying." I felt silly standing here at midnight talking to what my dad would see as an empty chair. But it wasn't empty. I knew that.

"I think," I tried again, "that you're really missing someone. Someone you love."

She rocked on. I couldn't tell whether she didn't hear me or was just ignoring me.

This is a waste, I thought. I stepped back, then

pictured the soldier. He was real. His sadness was real too. They needed my help.

I focused on the two of them. The pretty, slender woman with her long, honey-colored waves and the brave soldier in his smart uniform. I could imagine them as they used to be years ago.

Together.

"I saw him today," I blurted. "He's here—well, nearby—and he's looking for you. He misses you. Oh, and he's handsome, too."

I left out the part about his arm, in case she didn't know about his injury.

I waited, but she didn't answer. She cried and rocked in her chair, as if I wasn't there.

"I need you to ask for my help," I explained. "That's the only way it works." If a spirit didn't request your assistance, you were powerless no matter what you thought was best. I'd learned that when I'd once tried to help the spirit of Jayden's brother.

The young woman said nothing. She was lost in her own sorrow.

I waited as long as I could bear it, then left, closing the door behind me. I stood in the hall, shivering in my thin T-shirt and flannel boxers, too wound up to go back to bed.

Then I heard footsteps.

Lady Azura was prowling around downstairs.

Two slices of yellow cake with two forks were already set out when I reached the kitchen.

"Milk or lemonade?" Lady Azura asked. Her back was to me. She stared out the window into the darkness.

Still waiting.

"Milk," I answered. "How do you do that? Know when I'm coming?" She was always ready for me.

"You have strong energy." She brought the carton and sat beside me at the table.

The young woman's sobs drifted down the stairs, creating a background hum.

"You hear her, right?" I asked.

Lady Azura raised her eyes to the ceiling. "Sadness reminds you to appreciate happiness all the more."

"There's a lot of things to learn in this house." I thought of how the crying woman wouldn't talk to me. "A lot of things I don't know."

Lady Azura stopped chewing her cake and swallowed

hard. "We learn things when the time is right."

"But I want to be involved." I really did want to make the woman stop crying.

"He just can't tell you right now."

I realized we weren't both talking about the sad spirit upstairs. "Are you talking about my dad? What's going on with you two?"

Lady Azura sucked in her breath. "I can't say. I made a promise."

"A promise?" I was so frustrated. "It's not fair. I live here too." Then I blurted out what I'd been worrying about so much the last few days. "Do you want us out?"

"Out?" She seemed surprised. "No, of course not. I just . . . He and I don't . . ." She didn't finish. Shaking her head, she squeezed her eyes shut.

"Don't what?" My hands clenched into fists in front of me on the table. "I have a right to know if it has to do with my dad." Anger and frustration churned together inside me. The questions, the fear, and the doubt whirled around like a tornado, clouding my vision, making it impossible to focus. Lady Azura reached over and put her hands over mine.

Then I saw her.

A frail woman stood before me in a long black dress. A black hat with a black feather in front masked her face in shadows. I breathed in the sweet smell of freshly cut grass and damp earth and realized, oddly, that we were suddenly outside and it was summer. The woman's thin shoulders heaved up and down. With a shaky gloved hand, she brought a handkerchief up to her face to dab her eyes. Her hand knocked back the hat's brim, and I gasped.

"You!" I cried.

"Me, what?" Lady Azura asked.

I shook my head and blinked several times. Lady Azura sat in front of me wrapped in her white silk robe, yet I had just seen her outside, wearing black and weeping. A vision. I'd had a vision.

What did it mean?

Lady Azura was crying because she was at a funeral, I realized. I wanted to ask her about it, but I couldn't.

I was afraid to know who had died . . . or who was going to die.

Chapter 8

"You never told me what happened." Lily leaned forward, resting her head on the back of my chair. Her class had just filed into the row behind mine in the auditorium.

"Nothing much." I examined the snowflake I'd painted on my thumbnail with Wite-Out. If I turned to look at Lily, she'd know I was keeping stuff from her.

"Oh! Something big happened." She knew anyway. "Tell me."

"Tell you what?" Avery Apolito asked from the seat next to me.

"Sara and Dina went to the mall the other day," Lily explained.

"Together?" Avery scooted even closer.

"It's not a big deal," I said. I shifted my attention to the lines of kids streaming down the aisle next to me, filling up the auditorium, as if I was searching for someone.

He saw me looking when his class entered. My face flushed as he stopped alongside my seat.

"*Feliz Navidad.*" Jayden leaned on my armrest. I could smell the almond scent of his soap.

"*Joyeux Noël,*" I replied. I felt Lily's and Avery's eyes cataloging our every movement. I tried to pretend they weren't inches away.

"You read your handout, I see," Jayden said, waving the pale green flyer in his hand. It listed how to say "Merry Christmas" in ten languages. "And you wore a red sweater in honor of the Holidays Around the World assembly. Impressive display of school spirit."

"I try." I grinned. I loved the easy way we talked. "What happened to you? Brown is not very festive."

"I don't do red. Green is okay, though." He tapped his fingers on my armrest. "What's your favorite color?"

"Why?"

"I need to know. It's a surprise. Just answer."

"Blue."

"What kind of blue? Dark or light—"

"Hey, Mendes! You're causing a traffic jam," called a tall boy behind him.

"Keep moving!" shouted some other guy.

"Later," Jayden called to me, as he headed down the crowded aisle.

"He is so buying you a present!" Lily squealed.

"Shhh," I quieted her, although it did look that way. "Now what do I get him? I need major help here."

"A red shirt, for sure," Avery said. "That would be funny."

"It would." Should I go the funny route? I wasn't sure. I thought again about the old couple in the store. It was so sweet how he always got her the perfume.

"I don't think a T-shirt has enough meaning," Lily disagreed.

"It means she has a sense of humor," Avery countered. "Guys are into funny."

"But it doesn't say that Sara really likes Jayden," Lily pointed out.

"Sara likes Jayden?"

Lily, Avery, and I turned together. Dina Martino stood in her typical hands-on-hips pose in the aisle alongside me. Another eighth-grade girl stood beside her.

"It's Jayden who likes Sara," Lily countered. I couldn't believe Dina had overheard us talking about Jayden.

Dina eyed me thoughtfully, then smiled. "I think that's great, Sara. Jayden's really cute. Isn't he cute, Ava?"

"Totally." Ava nodded enthusiastically.

"Oh, hey, I'm liking the outfit." Dina pointed to the skinny multicolored scarf I'd wrapped around my neck. "Especially the scarf." She smiled at me again. A big, friendly smile. "See you later, Sara. Maybe after school?"

"Bye," Ava called. She followed Dina down the aisle, as the assistant principal tapped the microphone onstage for attention.

"What was *that*?" Avery exclaimed. "Dina is now your friend? How did that happen?"

"I'm not quite sure," I admitted. My finger found the opal among the gemstones and crystals on my necklace.

"That must've been some shopping trip," Lily

murmured, as the lights dimmed to start the assembly.

"Mouths closed, attention up front," a gray-haired teacher warned. "That's the rule."

I liked her rule. I was keeping my mouth closed. I wouldn't tell Lily and Avery what had happened at the mall, and I certainly wouldn't tell them what Dina and I were about to do.

I didn't know which they'd think was stranger: my talking to gummy bears or my agreeing to help Dina with her evil plan.

I was the first one out of school.

I'd told Lily I had to race home to help Lady Azura with chores. Not a total lie, because I did do that in the afternoons, but I was really avoiding Dina. I doubted she'd be so bold as to track me down at home.

"Hey!" I greeted the knitting woman on the porch. I was used to her always sitting there, never talking.

I entered the front foyer, and sobs floated down the stairs. The crying spirit.

The sobs sounded clearer today. Less muffled. I stood against the dark-wood banister and listened. They weren't all coming from upstairs, I realized with a start. Slowly I followed the noise down the narrow hallway, back toward the kitchen.

Why was the crying spirit downstairs? I wondered. Ever since I'd moved in, she'd never left her rocking chair in the pink bedroom.

Turned out it wasn't the crying spirit I was hearing.

I stopped in the doorway, unsure what to do. Should I back away? It felt wrong to stand there and watch.

"I'm fine," she said, not turning to me. "Come in."

I inched over, my eyes focused on the black-and-white photographs scattered on the table. Before I could make out any faces, she scooped them in a pile and tucked them into a yellowing envelope.

I'd seen Lady Azura cry only twice. Once in that vision and now again. Something bad must be going on.

"I'm sure Richard will come back. There's still five more days until Christmas," I told her.

"I'm not crying for Richard." She dabbed her smudged mascara with a paper napkin. "Richard always comes back on Christmas morning. Very early. Up with the birds." She smoothed her hair. "But he's not the only man I wait for."

"Really?" I sat next to her.

"Really." She pressed her bony hands together and pursed her lips. "When I graduated high school I met the most glorious young man. He worked at the shoe store. Let me tell you, I bought a lot of shoes that summer! Franklin was so handsome. The palest gray eyes, and smart! We talked for hours. We fell in love." She turned to stare out the window. "He was my first love. My true love."

"What happened?"

"Franklin proposed to me at the end of the summer, and we set a wedding date. December 22, 1944. We rented the hall. I shopped for a dress. We were so happy. We had such big plans."

"So you married him before you married Richard?"

"No. World War II was raging overseas, and Franklin was called up to the army that September. He died in battle. There was no wedding."

"I'm sorry." I wanted to reach out to her, pat her hand or something, but I wasn't sure if I should.

"He came back," she continued. "That December twenty-second, he came back to me. I put on my wedding dress, and we danced. All day we danced and laughed. And then he was gone again." She fumbled with the collar of her aqua silk blouse. "Every December twenty-second, though, Franklin came back to visit me. For over fifty years, we shared that one day together. I wait for that day every year."

"That's why your Advent calendar only goes to the twenty-second!" Now I understood. "So he'll be here in a few days." I wondered if I'd be able to see him too.

She shook her head. "He stopped coming ten years ago."

"Why? Was he jealous of your husband?"

"No. He came for years and years while Richard was alive, and Richard had been long gone when he stopped." She sighed. "I don't know why he stopped coming. I fear I've gotten too old for him. He remains forever a young man, and I have grown into an old woman with these horrid wrinkles."

"What? You look great." I meant it. Lady Aura was the most exotic, most fashionable old person I'd ever seen.

"Not great enough." She shook her head. "I keep waiting. Maybe this year . . ."

"Can't you summon him? Bring him here?" I'd seen

Lady Azura call back the spirits of the dead. She had the power to do it.

"Sometimes one needs to accept the way things are. My feelings are selfish. Until I can go to him, it must remain Franklin's choice."

She slid out the top photo from the envelope and pushed it toward me. "This is my Franklin."

He wore a plain white button-down shirt and dark pants and was posed with both hands in his pockets. He looked happier, less tired, more, well . . . alive than the last time I'd seen him, in the mall. Even though he wasn't wearing his uniform, I recognized him immediately. Franklin was the army guy.

I'd had it all wrong. The soldier wasn't looking for the crying spirit upstairs. He was looking for Lady Azura!

"Okay, enough about what's long gone." Lady Azura stood and pulled back her thin shoulders. "I need something to sweeten this day. Candy is the answer."

Candy was always her answer. But I had a different answer. An answer even sweeter than candy. I would surprise her and bring Franklin back to her.

Chapter 9

The ugly sweater with Mrs. Claus's smiling face was starting to look pretty good to me. At least, pretty warm, after I passed the Salty Crab's window display for the eighth time the next afternoon.

I zipped my parka up under my chin and pulled my wool hat over my ears. I'd been walking up and down Beach Drive for almost two hours, pretending to shop for presents.

I was really searching for Franklin.

I hoped he would be out here. Somewhere. It sure seemed as if every other spirit lurked about. Three older men in long overcoats on the corner of Dune Lane sang a harmonized "Silent Night" every time I passed. I was the only one who heard their ghostly song.

I looped around and started up the other side of the street. I dodged women with strollers and giggling groups of high school girls. The sidewalk was crowded with people out shopping the Friday before Christmas. I stared openly at each one and then slid my gaze sideways to the spirit that often hovered nearby. An old woman. An old man. A toddler, hurrying to catch up.

No Franklin.

I wished I knew a better way to find him.

He'd been here the first time I saw him, I reminded myself.

I thought about my talk with Lady Azura. Did Franklin have something to do with why she wanted Dad to move out? Or why I'd had that vision of her at a funeral? I couldn't figure out how they were all connected. Maybe if she wasn't so sad about Franklin, she'd tell me.

My phone buzzed. It was from a number I didn't recognize.

I ducked alongside the Seasons Sports window to read the text.

R WE ON 4 TOMORROW NITE? GOT 2 STOP THEIR TRIP!

I'd been avoiding Dina all week at school. Now she'd found me.

R U THERE???? NEED 2 PLAN NOW!!!!!

I continued down the street, reading Dina's texts. They kept coming, each more insistent than the next.

Finally I couldn't take it. Ignoring her wasn't working. I circled back and entered the Salty Crab. The small store was warm and smelled of candy canes.

"Sara! Have you come to shop? Where's Lily?" Aunt Delores called from behind the counter. She was wrapping a box with shiny gold paper.

"I'm by myself," I explained. "I need a present for Lily."

"Delightful!" Delores looked ready for Santa's workshop. She wore a red furry cap with a jingle bell on top, and her round cheeks were rosy. "Let me fishing wrapping these, and I'll be right there."

I scooted over to the table where the ugly pompom hat still lay. Figured. No one would ever buy it. At least, I hoped not. I could just imagine my dad thinking it was fun and surprising me with it. Luckily, this was not his kind of store. If they sold it in the hardware store, I'd be a goner.

Another text buzzed in. Dina.

IS THIS REALLY A GOOD IDEA? I texted back.

YES!!!!! U PROMISED. Her fingers must've been hovering over the phone, she texted back so fast.

Y DONT U WANT THEM 2GETHER? I wrote.

Did she not like my dad? I couldn't see why. He was a really nice guy. Good-looking in that rugged way. Maybe not the funniest sense of humor, but not horrible, either.

Wait. Maybe it's me, I thought. Did she want to break them up because she didn't like me?

NOT SHARING W U. U NEED 2 DO THIS. I WILL SHOW THAT VIDEO!!!!!

"Did you find something?" Delores pushed a stray auburn curl under her cap and hurried over.

I lifted the red-and-green hat.

"Oh, perfect! So fun! So Lily!" She reached for it. "Would you like it wrapped?"

"Thanks." As she returned to the counter, I stared at the flood of texts from Dina. Instructions on how to keep Dad from going to Philadelphia tomorrow with her mom.

I was so stupid! Why hadn't I made her erase that

video in the mall? Why had I thought I could trust her?

FINE. I'LL TRY, I wrote back. I didn't see that I had a choice.

I reached down for the Stellamar snow globe. The boardwalk with its Ferris wheel, arcade games, and haunted house were all squeezed inside the clear plastic dome. I shook it, watching the snow flutter. Inside, the town looked so peaceful and empty. No spirits trapped inside.

I squinted at the tiny arcade, remembering the time Jayden and I had sat so close in the photo booth. We'd been together in Lily's uncle's pizza place and her other uncle's ice-cream shop. I could make out both places inside the tiny globe.

A shiver suddenly tingled my neck, and the temperature around me plummeted. I hugged my arms around my chest and turned. Had someone opened the door, letting in the cold air?

The store was quiet. The door was closed. Delores wrapped away, not noticing the arctic drop.

I started to shake. A chill coursed through my body, turning my blood cold. Something was happening.

I closed my eyes. Tried to stop it. Tried to come up with a White Light. Something to block whoever was seeking me out.

"Oh, look! It's starting to flurry!" Delores exclaimed.

I opened my eyes and glanced out the door's glass window, and that was when I saw him hurry past.

Franklin!

"Can I come back later to get the present?" I asked, halfway to the door.

"Sure, I'll—" That was all I heard. Franklin was turning the corner, almost out of sight. I chased after him, weaving around shoppers and carolers.

He headed down a small side street I'd never noticed. The snow swirled about, sticking to my eyelashes, making it hard to see. Franklin moved fast, his feet always an inch above the ground. Never truly here on Earth.

The chill I'd felt had been him.

"Stop!" I called.

My voice was drowned out by the clanging of the Salvation Army volunteer's bell. I sidestepped around the collection pot, all the while keeping Franklin in sight. His body wasn't fully solid, but I could still track his khaki uniform in the sea of holiday red and green.

And then I couldn't.

A wall of bundled-up toddlers and parents, loaded down with cameras and bags of snack food, appeared at the next corner. Everyone pushed together, trying to get into what looked like an Italian restaurant.

"Excuse me! Excuse me!" I cried, trying desperately to slip through the crowd.

"Back of the line," a man with a clipboard called to me. "Santa's only taking pictures for another forty-five minutes, and these folks have been waiting."

"I just need to get through," I said. I'd lost sight of Franklin. "Please!"

A woman with twins holding on to both her hands made room, and I squeezed through. I ran down the next street. Searching, searching . . . for a ghost.

This was the first time I was looking for one of them instead of the other way around.

He seemed to have disappeared. I stopped running and stood, watching the snow blanket the sidewalk. My first snow. Maybe we would have a white Christmas. I sighed. Did it matter? How fun would it really be with Lady Azura so sad?

Then I got angry. What was with Franklin? What gave him the right to stop visiting her and cause her to cry?

"Franklin! Franklin!" I whirled about, screaming until I was hoarse.

"Over here." His voice was low. I had to shade my eyes to find him, waiting for me in a nearby doorway.

"You came," he said, when I squeezed next to him. A small overhang blocked the snow. "I didn't think you would."

"I had to chase you down."

"I didn't realize you were following me. I was trying to understand the streets." He raised his arms, as if giving up. "I never know where I am anymore."

"Where have you been?" I demanded. "You haven't shown up in ten years. Ten years! That's a long time."

"I know." His gray eyes drew me in. "I've been searching. . . ."

"Searching for what?"

"For her. For Azura." Once again, I could feel his frustration. His sense of loss.

"But she's lived in the same house for"—I realized I had no idea how long—"for a long time."

"But I can't find it anymore," he said, frustration obvious in his voice. "Everything in this town has changed. I left her in that house when I went off to war. She has always lived in the house she grew up in. I came back to that house every year. I followed the same streets every year to get there . . . and then one year I returned and couldn't find my way."

"Why not?" I raised my eyebrows at a woman watching me from across the street. I knew she couldn't see Franklin. I knew I appeared to be talking to the door. For once, I didn't care what some stranger thought. She could just mind her own business. I needed to help Lady Azura.

"The town built this enormous building with a hundred stores all inside it. The strangest thing, really. It takes up many, many blocks. When they built it ten years ago, they changed around the streets. Added new ones. Rerouted old ones. I don't have a map. My sense of direction is forever in 1944."

"The mall! You're talking about the mall," I said.

"Whatever that big place is, it's kept me from her."

He reached out to me with his one good hand. "I miss her so much."

No longer did I smell death on him. He smelled almost citrusy. And he sounded sincere.

"I can take you to her. I'll show you the way to the house!" I was so excited. "Let's go. I'll show you now."

Franklin's thin lips turned up into a smile. "Not now. It's not the right day. I must wait until the twenty-second."

"That's tomorrow." I thought ahead. "Tomorrow's Saturday. My dad will be away. Well, maybe . . . I don't actually know what's going to happen with that." I bit my lip, thinking. It would be better if my dad wasn't at the house. He didn't believe in spirits and visions. I couldn't imagine what he would do if Lady Azura started dancing with someone he couldn't see.

I made up my mind. I wouldn't stop Dad from going off with Janelle, even though I'd promised. I'd just have to find a way to deal with Dina and the video.

"You have to come tomorrow," I told Franklin. "My dad will be in Philadelphia, so you and Lady Azura can be alone. You can spend the day together like you used to." I glanced up at the street sign. "Meet me here tomorrow at eleven in this exact spot, and I'll show you the way."

Chapter 10

His bag was packed, waiting at the top of the stairs, but Dad sat on the sofa in our second-floor family room, pretending to read a magazine.

Why wasn't he leaving?

I watched him flip the pages. Glance at an article, then at his watch. Glance at a picture, then at his watch.

I sat at the large table that used to be in our old kitchen and clicked through photos on my camera, looking for ones to run with the story on the library and another story about the new trophy case.

I glanced at the screen, then at Dad. Screen and then at the clock. Ten thirty a.m.

Neither of us spoke. No one moved.

Dad lifted his cell phone and texted.

He groaned when he saw the answer and texted some more.

I looked at the clock again. 10:35 a.m. In twenty-five minutes, I had to meet Franklin. Dad should've been gone by now.

"What time's the wedding?" I asked.

"Two." He rubbed his fingers alongside his temples. I knew that move. He was stressed. "We may not go, though. Dina's not feeling well."

Of course she's not, I thought. "What's wrong with her?"

"Janelle says she has stomach pains."

"You could go to the wedding by yourself," I suggested.

"I don't know. I'd feel bad leaving Janelle here." He shook his head. "She got a new dress and everything."

"I'm sure it's real pretty." *Probably pink,* I thought.

"I guess I could stay around and replace some of the rotting floorboards. Have you heard how they creak?"

"You don't want to do that." I couldn't have him hanging out all day. "Wouldn't your friend want you to go to his wedding? I mean, didn't you promise?"

"I did." Dad started texting Janelle again. "Maybe I can convince Janelle that Chloe can take care of Dina. She seems very responsible, don't you think?"

Now my phone buzzed. Dina.

WHATS HAPPENING? MOM WAS GOING 2 STAY BUT YOUR DAD KEEPS PUSHING. STOP HIM!!!

"Chloe's only sixteen," I said halfheartedly.

"Dina could come over here," he suggested.

Oh no, she can't! I thought. "It's probably not a good day. Lady Azura's going to be sad today."

"Really?" He put down his phone. "Why?"

"Did you know that she was engaged and her fiancé died in World War II? Today would've been her wedding day. Well, her first wedding day." I explained about Franklin and what had happened. Of course, I left out that he came back every year and that his spirit was waiting for me in town.

"She really loved him a lot," I told Dad.

"She loved Richard, too."

"You know about Richard?" I was surprised. Dad and Lady Azura's only conversations seemed to be about house repairs and what to buy at the market.

"Um, she told me about him. They traveled a lot together. All over South America and to Australia." He paused. "She said it was his idea that she open a fortune-telling business. As I take it, they were both a bit offbeat." He chuckled.

"But he wasn't her *first* love," I reminded him. "You told me how special a first true love is."

"I did. It is." Dad patted the cushion, and I curled up beside him. "There are many kinds of love, kiddo. First loves come only once. Some of us are lucky enough to have our first love with us our entire lives. Others—like Lady Azura and me—lose that love, but that doesn't mean we lose the ability to love." He reached for my hand. "There are other loves, different loves for different times in our life. People need love."

"What about you?"

"Me too." He took a deep breath, considering. "Janelle and I need more time together for me to know what comes next, but it would be nice to find love again."

Now *my* stomach hurt. I could ruin this chance for him.

If I said I didn't feel well either, that would be it. With two sick kids, they'd cancel the trip. Dina would get what she wanted. At least for this weekend.

And my dad would be lonely.

And I would feel guilty.

If I could separate Janelle from her daughter, she wasn't all that bad. I wished I could separate them. Keep Dina away.

I twisted the silver cord of my necklace around my finger, then raised the crystals to inspect them. Next to the opal, the aquamarine crystal glowed in the morning light. The aquamarine was supposed to give me courage.

Did I have the courage to go up against Dina?

I hoped so.

"You should convince Janelle to go with you," I said. "Really, I mean it. Dina was fine at school yesterday. I think she's probably just being dramatic because she wants her mom to stay home and take her Christmas shopping or something like that. I'm sure she'll be okay." I chewed my lip, then said, "And if she is really sick, she can come over here and rest if she wants to."

"You're the best, kiddo." Dad gave me a hug. His cheek was stubble free and smooth. He'd shaved for Janelle, even though he hated to shave on the weekends.

He took his phone and wandered down the hall to his bedroom to call Janelle.

I checked the clock again. 10:50.

I wondered if I could tell Dad I needed to go into town for something. What? More presents? I'd already used that excuse yesterday. I wandered to the window. Yesterday's snow had turned to slush. The bay water in the distance looked flat and gray.

How long would Franklin wait? I wondered.

I fiddled with my phone. I couldn't call someone who wasn't living. He didn't even know what a cell phone was, I realized. I looked around the room—at the flat-screen TV, Dad's laptop, my iPod. He wouldn't know any of these things. He didn't even know where to find the house.

Everything changed, I realized. Except love.

Franklin still loved Lady Azura.

The way the old man in the store loved his wife.

The way I hoped my mom somewhere loved my dad.

"I'm off!" Dad announced as he came back into the room. He looked much happier. "Janelle and I are dropping Dina and Chloe at their aunt's house. She should be fine. Janelle says the stomachache comes and goes."

"That's great, Dad." It made me happy to see him so happy.

"I wrote down the phone number of where I'm staying, and you have my cell. Lady Azura should be up and about soon." He glanced at the clock. 11:10. "Well. Almost noon." We usually didn't see her before noon on the weekends. She said she needed time to "put on her face," which meant all the makeup and creams she wore.

I decided to ask. "Is everything okay with you and Lady Azura?"

"Us? Oh, we're fine. Just a little disagreement. We're working on solving it." He was trying way too hard to sound casual.

"What's it about?"

"Nothing to worry about. We made a deal when we moved in, and she was looking for a way out."

"A way out?"

"No worries, Sara, I'm figuring through things, finding a way to move forward."

There was that word again. *Move.*

He pointed to the clock. "Janelle's waiting."

I didn't want to let him run out on this conversation. Dad was a master avoider. But Franklin was waiting too. At least, I hoped so.

"Will you tell me about it when you come home?"

"We'll talk. I promise." He took hold of his bag. "Listen, do me a favor. Lay off the questions with Lady Azura when I'm gone, okay?"

"Questions about what?" I asked. "Neither of you will say what's going on."

Dad smiled and gave me a kiss on my cheek.

My phone buzzed even before he reached the bottom stair.

U MESSED IT ALL UP!!! R U NUTS?

I tucked it back into my jeans pocket. I didn't want to reply. Maybe I *was* nuts. I could only imagine how miserable Dina was going to make my life at school.

But with the holidays, I was off from school until after New Year's. For all I knew, Dad would tell me we were moving by then. Moving forward. Moving away.

Was it the same thing?

I put the awful thought out of my mind. I had to get to Franklin.

I waited until I saw Dad's car drive up the street, then hurried downstairs. I grabbed my navy parka from the brass rack near the door and searched the pockets for gloves.

"Where are you off to? It's frigid out today."

I stared at Lady Azura. She still wore her white silk robe. Her mahogany-dyed hair was covered by an emerald-green scarf wrapped up like a turban. She looked pale, tired, and wrinkled. No makeup, no perfume, stray gray hairs poking out around her temples.

"Are you okay?" I asked, alarmed at the puffiness of her eyes. She'd been crying again.

"Yes." She reached for the large opal on the chain around her neck and cupped her palm over it. "It's just one of those days."

"I was just going into town quickly to get, um"—I searched for an excuse—"the present I bought for Lily. The Salty Crab was wrapping it. I can bring something back from the bakery. That'll give you time to get dressed," I offered.

"Oh, I'm not going to get dressed today."

"You're not?" I'd never seen her not get dressed.

"Today is a wrap-myself-in-blankets-and-watch-movies day. You can go to town later. Let's watch *Breakfast at Tiffany's*. Audrey Hepburn is divine in it."

"But I need to get Lily's present."

She waved her hand and grunted. "Delores isn't going anywhere. She'll have it tomorrow."

I shifted my weight from foot to foot. Lady Azura wanted to watch movies with me. She looked frail and vulnerable, and I knew I should keep her company.

But I knew why she'd been crying. Today was the day. December 22. I could fix everything. I had the power to bring Franklin back to her.

"I promised I'd be there today. Now." I slipped on my jacket and gloves. "I'll go really quick and then come back for the movie. And I'll bring back a surprise for you."

"Chewy candy. Nothing chocolate."

"Sure." She thought the surprise was candy for the movie. She had no idea. "Are you sure you don't want to put something else on? You always talk about that

Audrey actress's style. Why don't you dress up like her?"

"I'll admire it on screen. I don't have it in me today. Not today." She turned back toward her bedroom.

I raced through the slushy streets of Stellamar. I had to hurry. I had to find Franklin. I'd never seen Lady Azura so defeated, so heartbroken. She was the one who stayed strong when I was scared. She was the one who fixed what went wrong.

It was my turn now.

Icy water seeped into my sneakers, soaking my socks, as I rounded the road leading onto Beach Drive. A cold rain began to fall. I skidded down the street, dodging the umbrellas now opening. Strands of my hair, plastered with rain, stuck to my cheeks.

It was after 11:40 when I reached the side street. I stopped at the doorway, searching. He wasn't there.

The street was empty. No people—dead or alive. Rain drummed against a metal garbage can by the curb. I waited, my heart thumping along with the beat of the drops.

I waited and waited.

He didn't appear.

Was I too late, or had he decided not to show?

I had wanted so much to bring him and Lady Azura back together. Now I'd failed.

"Franklin!" I shouted into the storm. "Franklin!"

Chapter 11

A woman walking a shaggy dog in a yellow rain slicker stopped at the corner, as I screamed Franklin's name over and over. I turned my back to her and debated what to do next.

Search the streets for him? Pick up Lily's present and lots of candy and go home?

Rain dripped into my eyes, and the gloves' wet wool stuck to my fingers. "Franklin!" I cried for the last time.

"Over here."

I whirled around and whooped. He was there, shimmering in the doorway. I didn't ask where he'd been. He could've been anywhere. I was so happy to see him.

He stood, completely dry in his uniform, while the rain poured down.

"Is she waiting for me?" His low voice wavered, unsure.

I thought of Lady Azura in her bathrobe with her puffy eyes. "Yes." I hoped he wouldn't be disappointed when he saw her. "Actually, she doesn't know. It's a surprise. You're the perfect Christmas present."

He liked that and followed me through the wet streets. I made him detour to the Salty Crab. I quickly picked up Lily's present and, on a whim, used some of the money Dad had given me to buy one of those Stellamar snow globes.

When we reached the house, I stopped him on our porch. Franklin didn't seem to notice the knitting lady. Maybe the dead couldn't see one another?

"Wait here," I told him.

I entered and peeled off my coat and gloves. Kicking my wet sneakers aside, I padded toward the clanking of dishes in the kitchen.

"Oh, child, you are drenched." Lady Azura stood by the stove with a coffee mug in her hand. "Go upstairs and put on something cozy."

She was still wearing her bathrobe. The overhead light of the kitchen illuminated the wrinkles she was so worried about Franklin seeing.

I couldn't tell her to put on makeup without ruining the surprise. I thought about Franklin.

He loved her. He wanted to see her. I didn't think he'd care what she looked like. Besides, if he were alive he'd have wrinkles too. Lots of them.

"Sara, did you hear me? Don't just stand there dripping."

"I have a surprise for you."

"Later. Go change. I'll make hot chocolate."

"Now," I insisted. I reached for her hand. "It's a Christmas present, but you need to see it today."

I led her down the hall and flung open the door. Franklin reached out his hand to her.

Lady Azura didn't move. She didn't speak. Her gaze drifted past him to the street and a silver car splashing through the puddles.

Did she not see him?

Could only I see Franklin?

"I've found my way back." Franklin's voice was heavy with hope.

Lady Azura stared silently into the distance.

"Do you see him?" I whispered.

She began to tremble, and her eyes grew wide. "It's not my imagination then?"

"I brought him here."

She fell into him, wrapping her arms around his translucent body, hugging him as tightly as if he was made of stone. "It's you, it's you," she repeated.

Then I heard her giggle. No longer an old woman. This was the giggle of an eighteen-year-old girl.

Franklin hugged her back, murmuring in her ear. He clearly didn't care how she looked. I had the feeling he saw her as he'd left her so many years ago.

Lady Azura ushered him into the house, and they beamed at each other. Her pale skin glowed with her happiness. I felt silly standing there. They had only today together. I was sure they didn't want to spend it with me.

"I'm going to change clothes," I announced. "And then I'm going over to Lily's."

"Are you sure?" Lady Azura suddenly seemed flustered. "Your dad thinks I'm watching you—"

"Mrs. Randazzo's expecting me. It's all planned out," I assured her.

"You did this?" Her voice rose in amazement. "How

did you find him? I haven't taught you how yet—"

"He found me," I explained. "All I had to do was listen." Then, with a quick hug good-bye, I left the room and left Lady Azura alone with Franklin.

Lily's house was Christmas Central.

Pine garlands decorated the doorways, and Mrs. Randazzo's collection of Santa figurines covered the tops of each table. Dozens of stockings in every fabric imaginable were clipped to clotheslines zigzagging across the family room. Lily's brothers' loud voices competed with the newest pop Christmas carol on the radio, and the aroma of sugar and butter wafted from the kitchen.

Mrs. Randazzo put me to work sprinkling crystallized sugar over cutout cookies. Aunt Angela and Aunt Susan prepared the dough, and Lily, her little sister, Cammie, and two cousins used the cookie cutter and the rolling pins.

"Did you hear that Fred's getting Michelle that diamond necklace?"

"Get out! The tacky one in the window at Jems and Jewels?"

"That's the one. Michelle doesn't know. She was wanting the one with the blue stone. Fred brought his mother to pick it out."

"My Joey's mother wouldn't know a diamond from a Brillo pad."

"That's why Joey got you another set of pots and pans!"

"With a diamond finish, you know it!"

The three women cracked up laughing. All afternoon, the aunts and cousins told stories, gossiped, and teased one another. I wasn't truly part of the family, but I pretended I was. I laughed about Fred and Joey and took sides when they debated about which fish to serve on Christmas Eve.

I'd never been surrounded by so many people related to one another. They were loud and crazy and fun.

"Sara, sweetie, what's your family making for Christmas?" Aunt Angela asked, after they'd gone over their elaborate menu.

"Dad said we'd get a ham this year," I said. "And mashed potatoes. He likes to make those."

"Who all comes over?" Angela leaned toward me,

and I noticed her flawless French manicure was caked with dough.

"Usually it's just us two. Me and Dad." I paused. "And I think Lady Azura this year."

If she and Dad stop fighting, I thought.

"Where's the rest?" Sophia, Lily's ten-year-old cousin, asked.

"There's no rest. I mean, there's my dad's sister, Charlotte, and my uncle Dexter, but they live in California still. My dad's dad, Gramp Steve, is kind of sick. He lives in a special place that takes care of old people out there. We never really see him."

"What about your mom's family?" Angela asked. She handed a stack of dirty bowls to Lily's mom at the sink.

I shrugged and moved to help Mrs. Randazzo wash. "There's not any."

"Everyone has family," Angela said.

"Some of us have too much!" Lily teased.

"Lily, be nice!" Mrs. Randazzo scolded. She playfully flicked soapsuds toward her daughter.

"Not me," I explained. "My mom's mom died when she was in college. I think her dad died before that.

She didn't have any brothers or sisters—"

"Like you," Lily pointed out.

"Yep." I passed Mrs. Randazzo a handful of cookie cutters to rinse. "Anyway, everyone on that side is dead."

Mrs. Randazzo shut off the water and turned to face me. She held the dirty cookie cutters in her hand. "Maybe not everything is as it seems," she said in a soft voice.

"What?" I wasn't sure I'd heard her.

"What's that supposed to mean, Mom?" Lily asked, wrinkling her nose.

Mrs. Randazzo looked at me for a long time before answering. "You understand, Sara, don't you? Sometimes it takes a special person to see and listen."

Did I understand? I wasn't sure.

I was over their house a lot. Had Lily's mom somehow pieced together all my weirdness? Did she know I could talk to the dead?

"Really, Mom! You're freaking Sara out. Stop speaking like you're in your yoga Zen class." Lily tugged my sweater. "Let's get out of here." She headed toward the family room.

"We can shake all the presents and guess what's inside," Sophia suggested, as she and their cousin Ally followed.

I waited beside Mrs. Randazzo. Was I supposed to say something?

"Go on, Sara." She started to turn the faucet back on, then hesitated and spoke to me in a low voice so no one else would hear. "I . . . I'm here for you if you ever want to talk to someone, okay?"

I hesitated, unable to leave her side. I wanted to ask what she meant.

I reached for another dough-crusted cookie cutter lying on the counter. An angel with outstretched wings. I picked it up and felt the room spin.

The kitchen went dark, and suddenly Lady Azura stood by my side, dressed all in black. She wore a black hat with a feather. Her shoulders shook, and she let out a cry of anguish. I looked down at my hands, and I was no longer holding the cookie cutter, but a small porcelain angel instead. The angel looked so familiar to me. Something tugged at the edges of my memory, but the thought stayed just out of my grasp.

The fragile angel tumbled out of my hands and shattered.

Jagged pieces covered the ground, littering the grass at my feet.

Broken.

"Sara, are you crying?" Lily's mom surprised me.

I blinked and felt tears. I was back in the Randazzos' kitchen. The cookie cutter was in my hand. The tiled kitchen floor was empty.

"What's wrong?" Mrs. Randazzo spoke with such obvious concern for me that it made me want to cry even harder.

"Just—just thinking about something," I said lamely.

Another vision. I'd had another vision I didn't understand. Lady Azura was there again. Dressed in black.

Someone had died.

What was the deal with that angel?

"Gingerbread house time!" Sophia called from the next room.

"Coming, Sara?" Lily popped her head in the doorway.

"Do you want to go home?" Mrs. Randazzo asked me softly.

Lady Azura and Franklin were probably waltzing by our Christmas tree right now. Was I seeing images of Franklin's death? His funeral?

If so, why was *I* there?

"I love it here," I assured Mrs. Randazzo.

I walked slowly into the other room, willing myself to get swept up in the holiday excitement that bounced off Lily and her cousins.

But all the while, something nagged at me. Something I couldn't put my finger on. But it was there, just out of reach.

Chapter 12

I was up in my crafts room, gluing the final shell on Dad's box, when the doorbell rang Sunday morning.

"*I'm dreaming of a White Christmas . . .*" floated up as I made my way downstairs. It was the guy with the deep voice who sang on all Lady Azura's records. The music drifted out from under the double French doors leading to the sitting room. Those doors were rarely shut. Lady Azura must be inside, I realized. I hadn't seen her yet this morning. I wondered if Franklin was still in there with her.

I pushed back the faded curtains and peered out the small window by the front door. Jayden!

He stood on our porch with his hands plunged deep in his jacket pockets. I looked closer. No present. Maybe Lily had been wrong.

I pulled a hair band from around my wrist and twisted my messy hair into a ponytail. Luckily, I'd already changed out of pj's and into sweats.

"Hi," I said as I opened the door to a rush of cold air.

"Hi." He looked uncomfortable.

I didn't know what to say next. It was strange having him standing at my door on a Sunday.

"It's really cold out." He kicked his sneakers together.

"Oh. Right. You can come in." I opened the door wider.

"And dream of sleigh bells in the snow," the man continued to sing.

"Who is it?" Lady Azura's raspy voice rose over the music.

"Jayden," I called. I could hear the tinkle of ornaments being rearranged on the tree inside. I kept the double doors closed in case Franklin was around. Not that Jayden could see him, but still. It was better not to mix the living with the dead.

Jayden stood awkwardly in the front foyer. "We're going to Atlanta tonight."

"Right." That was weird. He could've texted me

good-bye. "Well, have a great trip."

"Yeah." He swept his fingers through the piece of hair that always fell across his forehead. He seemed to be working up the courage to say or do something. *Maybe there is a present,* I thought. Suddenly I realized that I *did* want him to give me something.

He was so cute, so nice.

"Dina sent me something this morning. A video of you. . . ."

My stomach dropped. She'd done it. She'd really done it.

He dug his phone out of his pocket, scrolled down a bit, then turned it toward me.

And there I was—talking to a spoonful of gummy bears.

"I—I—" What could I say? My brain scrambled through several different options. All lame.

I felt Jayden watching me. How could I have thought that he was getting me a present? No cute boy would buy something for a freaky girl like me. He'd probably sent the video on to his whole soccer team.

I raised my eyes. The corners of his mouth edged upward, holding back his laughter.

Great, I thought. *He came all the way over here to laugh at me.*

"It's awesome," he said, his face breaking into a smile.

"It is?"

"Totally. It's wicked how you play with Dina's mind. How you talk to the gummy bears like you really mean it." He laughed. "You totally freaked Dina out, and man, someone needed to freak that girl out."

"So you thought it was funny?" I wanted to be sure. Really sure.

"Hilarious!" He reached his hand up for a high five.

I slapped his hand, blushing when we touched.

"How many others did she send it to?" I was afraid to know.

Jayden shrugged. "Nobody, I think. She said it was just for me. She said I should 'watch and reconsider.'"

"Reconsider what?"

Now it was his turn to blush. "I guess liking you. She knew about that somehow."

"Oh." He did like me!

"Do you want me to delete it? I will."

I thought about it. If Jayden found it funny, others

would too. Kids at school thought Jayden was really cool. Dina's mean friends would tease me about it, but I'd be okay with Jayden and Lily by my side.

"Not really," I said. "It doesn't much matter."

"Good. I'm going to keep it."

He wanted to keep the video because I was in it, I realized. Not to make fun of me, but because he liked it because I was in it. Because he liked me.

Then he reached back into his jacket pocket, pulled out a small box wrapped in red-and-white paper, and handed it to me.

The present! I stared nervously at it for a moment. It was my first present from a boy.

"Should I open it now?" The paper was puckered, and lots of clear tape held the ends closed. He'd definitely wrapped it himself.

"If you want." He was having trouble looking at me. His eyes danced around the entryway, finally landing on an old framed photograph of the Stellamar boardwalk and beach from the 1930s that hung over the narrow table in the hall.

I tore the wrapping paper and pulled out a slim, pale-blue enamel picture frame.

"Because you're always taking pictures," Jayden explained in a rush as I studied the frame.

"It's so great . . . and it's blue."

"Yeah. There were lots of color choices. But your eyes are light blue, so I thought you'd like that."

"I do." I was blushing again. I already knew the photo I'd put inside. I'd taken it at a school soccer game. Of Jayden, of course.

"I have a present for you, too, but I didn't get to wrap it yet. Wait here." I ran back up to my crafts room. I still held the blue frame in my hand. I glanced at the wall where more of my mother's photographs hung, each in a thin silver frame. I'd taped a few of my photos next to hers. A swirly shell reflecting the glow of the setting sun. An overflowing trash can on the boardwalk.

Like her, I used to only photograph objects.

But that had changed in Stellamar. I was glad I had the photo of Jayden to go in his frame.

I reached for the snow globe that lay on a pile of colored paper and hurried back downstairs. Jayden said he really liked it. He kept shaking it, causing a blizzard to engulf our town.

Lady Azura's off-key voice carried into the hall. She was trying to harmonize with her favorite singer—whose name, I'd learned from my dad, was Frank Sinatra.

"Wow," Jayden said. "She sounds . . ."

"Happy," I filled in. Things must've gone well with Franklin.

"Well, I have to take off now," Jayden said, moving toward the door. In one quick movement, he leaned over and kissed me lightly on the cheek. And then he bolted out the door, turning once he was several paces away to yell, "Merry Christmas, Sara!"

I stood at the door, smiling a big goofy smile.

Later, after my heartbeat slowed back down, I pushed open the doors to the sitting room. Lady Azura was dressed in a silver lamé top and a long gold skirt. She looked even more sparkly than our tree. Her eyes sparkled too.

"Is Franklin still here?" I glanced around.

"No, his visits last only one day. One glorious day." She reached into a box of ornaments and began to unwrap the tissue paper around one. "He'll be back next year and the next until I'm no longer here. All thanks to you."

"You know, he scared me at first, when I didn't know who he was," I admitted. "But once I figured it out, I was happy to help."

"You help me in many ways." She smiled and handed me a glass ball etched with hummingbirds. "Hang this, will you?"

I placed the delicate ornament on the tree. "This is nice. So much prettier than those multicolored balls Dad bought and the ornaments I made at school when I was little." I pointed to the box. "Are these all yours?"

"Mine and Richard's." She unwrapped another. "Silly, really, all these birds, but that was Richard's passion." She held up a frosted-glass bluebird whose beak shimmered with silver glitter. "I haven't taken these out in many, many years. We had such a beautiful tree and right in this spot."

She hummed along with the music as she unwrapped and I hung the ornaments. "This one we bought the year my daughter was born." She held up a baby bird hatching from a turquoise speckled egg. The bird was decorated with tiny crystals.

"What was she like?"

"My daughter loved the outdoors—always hiking, skiing, and boating." She shook her head. "Diana was smart but oh, so practical. To her, the world was black and white. We had trouble together, because I inhabited the gray areas, and Diana didn't want gray areas in her life."

"The gray areas?"

"That which is not easily explained."

"Does that mean your daughter couldn't do what you do?"

"Did she have our power? No. She was always her father's daughter." She touched the baby bird. "Diana died in a boating accident when she was only forty-six. Far too young." Lady Azura placed the ornament gently on the tree. "She and Richard would be happy to see a tree up and decorated. It's been too long."

"They both come back then?"

"Richard comes back every Christmas Day. Diana visits less frequently. She often visits me in my dreams. I think she prefers it that way."

"Oh, can you convince her to come on Christmas so I can see her? I'd like to meet her. And Richard, of course."

Lady Azura stiffened. She pressed her lips together. "No, no, I think not."

"But I saw Franklin, so why not them?"

"They're just for me. It would better if you didn't . . . well, you'll be with your father that day. . . ." She fumbled for words. What was up? Why didn't she want me to see them?

"I won't say anything to Richard about Franklin," I promised.

"Oh, Richard knows about Franklin. Of course, he never knew for all those years that Franklin came back to see me, but a woman must have her secrets." She let out a frustrated sigh. "There are always secrets. Too many secrets." She lifted an iridescent bird from the box. "Look, it matches my necklace."

"You can take that off now." The opal still hung around her neck. "Franklin came back."

She rested a fingertip on the shiny stone. "He wasn't the wish this opal's being used for."

"You have another wish?"

"A better wish. An even more important wish."

"More important than finding your true love? What is it?"

"Secrets, like truths, must remain close to your heart." Lady Azura pointed to the box. "All done, and the tree looks beautiful. A bit birdy, perhaps, but beautiful."

"Wait, we missed one." An object wrapped in yellowed tissue rested on a side table.

"Oh no, that's not for this tree. That ornament came from Franklin."

"He brought you an ornament last night?"

"No. He sent it to me from Germany while he was away at war. It was to be a Christmas present. By the time it arrived, we had already been informed by the war office that Franklin had been killed in battle." She walked over to the table. "For years, I couldn't even look at this ornament. It wasn't until Diana's death that I was able to appreciate and hold on to its beauty. Only then did I hang it at the holidays."

"What does it look like?"

"It's a Christkindl. She's from an old German legend. The folklore says that she enters homes through a keyhole on Christmas Eve to bring toys to children."

"Kind of like Santa," I said, "but without the chimney."

"Exactly." Lady Azura smiled. "It was made by a man in a German village Franklin passed through. Franklin was so taken with it when he saw it. The detail in the painting is meticulous. He knew it would speak to me. Since I was a young girl, I've gravitated toward the different, the unique, that which no one else has."

"May I see it?"

"Of course, especially since Franklin now counts you as one of his favorite people."

Slowly I peeled back layer after layer of brittle tissue until the face of the Christkindl appeared. Round rosy cheeks. Wide blue eyes. A shiny gold crown resting on blond curls.

I stripped back the rest of the paper and perched the porcelain angel on my palm. I marveled at her golden wings and long white dress. A fine paintbrush and a steady hand had recreated detailed embroidery around the hem and along the sleeves.

I stared at her.

She was the angel.

The same angel I'd held and then dropped to the ground in my vision.

I turned her about in my hand. She was solid. No cracks. I felt as if she was looking right at me with her painted eyes. And then I realized something.

She *had* been watching me.

She'd been watching me since I was born.

I raced out of the room, the little angel still in my hand, and took the steps two at a time.

"Sara! Sara!" Lady Azura called to me, but I didn't stop.

I reached my room and stood staring at the wall, at the framed photos. The photos I'd had since I was a baby. Photos taken by my mother. Her name—Natalie Collins—was signed at the bottom of each one.

And there she was.

The one-of-a-kind Christkindl ornament all the way from Germany.

Lady Azura's angel ornament.

The ornament she'd had since 1944.

The ornament that was now in my hand.

So how could *my mother* have taken a photograph of it?

How did my mother know Lady Azura?

Chapter 13

"I'm home!" Dad called.

I couldn't stop looking, first at the photograph, then at the ornament. Back and forth until there was no doubt. They were the same. Exactly the same.

I sat on the floor, suddenly too exhausted to move.

I heard Dad's heavy footsteps climbing the stairs.

My mom and Lady Azura.

No one had said anything. Ever.

Secrets.

"Hi, kiddo! How was the weekend?" Dad bounded in and bent down to kiss me.

I didn't speak. Didn't look up. I cradled the little angel like a baby, letting his lips rest briefly on my head.

"Whatcha got there?" He squatted to look in my

hands, then followed my gaze to the wall. He inhaled sharply.

"It's not random that we're living in this house, is it?" I asked.

"No." He let his breath out with a rush.

I turned to face him. "Who is Lady Azura?"

He hesitated, and in that instant, I knew. He looked so uncomfortable and so worried, and I hated seeing him like that, but I had to hear him say it.

"Who is she?" I repeated my question.

"Lady Azura is your great-grandmother." His words hung in the air. "She's your mother's grandmother."

How could that be? My mind was churning. It didn't make sense. "B-but you said they were all dead."

Dad ran his hands through his hair. "Technically, I didn't say *all*. I only told you about your mom and your grandparents."

"Technically?" I cried. "So you just left out Lady Azura? Just like that? *For twelve years?*"

"Look, Sara, I might have made a mistake. I can see that now." He placed his hand on my shoulder. "I'm sorry, but things were different back then, back when you were born."

"Different how?" I demanded. "I'm not understanding this at all! How can she be my great-grandmother?" I thought back on the all the afternoons we'd spent together. Just the two of us. "Does she know?"

"Of course. She's always known." His voice was shaky.

"And you both kept this colossal secret from me? Why? Why would you do that to me?"

"When you were born . . ." Dad stopped. "Wait here." He walked out, and then I heard him rustling about in a room down the hall. The room he used for storage.

I felt numb. I just couldn't wrap my mind around the secret they'd kept from me.

"This will help to explain," Dad said, returning with a shoe box. He sat cross-legged on the floor beside me and opened the lid. The box was filled with letters and photos and cocktail napkins and other mementos. "These all have to do with your mom."

I could only stare at the box.

"But first, read this letter." He lifted a card off the top and handed it to me.

"What's this?" I ran my finger over the glittery

snowflakes on the blue background and the silver *Happy Holidays!* written across the top. A thick folded letter was contained inside the card.

"A letter I received last Christmas from Lady Azura," he explained. "It's what made me move us out here."

I unfolded the pages and read about the vision Lady Azura had about my mom, about her death and the guilt and arguments that followed, and about how Lady Azura knew, even across the country, that I had powers like she did.

When I was finished reading, my cheeks were damp with tears. I looked up and saw my dad was crying too.

"Why didn't you tell me? Either of you? We've been living here since the summer." My voice came out a whisper.

"It was my idea not to tell you. Blame me, Sara, not her. That's what we've been arguing about. She was angry with me for forcing her to keep it a secret. She was uncomfortable keeping the truth from you." He reached over and tucked a stand of hair behind my ears, the way he'd always done when I was little. "I never wanted to deceive you. I just wanted to protect you. I was afraid you'd get hurt if I suddenly introduced a great-grandmother and then had to take her away if things didn't work out."

"What things?"

He raised his hands. He looked so helpless. "I had no idea what would happen with Lady Azura. She's not your conventional grandmother. No knitting and baking cookies for her. She's always been kind of out-there and wacky, and I didn't know how you would react to her." He paused. "Or how I would react to her."

"What *do* you think of her?"

"I think she's great. I was wrong to jump to conclusions about her. I was wrong to keep you two apart." He tilted his head to the side and looked at me. "You like her too, right?"

I nodded. "She understands me."

"Better than I do?"

"In a different way." I stared at my socks. "We're very alike." I looked up and met his eyes. "We see the same things, Dad."

"I know." He looked uncomfortable, but not as uncomfortable as I had always imagined every time I'd thought about telling him. "I want you to talk to me, too. I know you see things, Sara. I may not understand it, but I'll listen and try to help. Will you talk to me? No matter what, I will always love you."

"I will tell you things from now on," I promised. *He knows,* I thought. *He knows!* I could feel my lungs expand. I felt as if I'd been holding my breath for years.

"I thought you were happy here, but if you're not . . . well, do you want to go back to California?" he asked. "I just want you to be happy, Sara."

Did I want to go back? I didn't even have to think about it. Good things happened here. Back in California, I was petrified to go to unfamiliar places and encounter spirits. Here I was beginning to understand my powers. I interacted with spirits and helped them. I'd met Lily, and already she was my best friend. I'd met Jayden, and he liked me. I felt at home in this house, and I loved my crafts room. I'd even gotten used to the crying spirit. She was like one of those crazy relatives people always complain about.

And most importantly, I had Lady Azura. She was a huge reason life was better.

"You like it here, right?" I asked Dad. "You like

your job, you like repairing this house, and you like Janelle."

"I do, but I love you more than all that. I'll do what's best for you."

"I want to stay." I was sure about that. "But what about Lady Azura? Does she want us here? She didn't seem like she did."

"She was just angry with me for not being straight with you. She wants you here more than anything." He got up slowly. "This was all her idea, Sara. You know, she's probably anxiously waiting downstairs to talk to you. I'm sure she has a lot to say."

She could tell me about my mom, I realized. All about her. And about me. She knew how we all fit together.

I had so many questions.

But for some reason, I was scared to talk to her.

Would things change between us, now that I knew?

"I don't want to go down there yet," I told him.

"Take your time." He walked to the door. "Why don't you look through the box, then come find me? I have many stories that I've kept to myself for far too long."

I promised I'd come to his room soon.

I shifted through the contents of the box. A program from my parents' wedding. A tarot card with the picture of a sun. A wrapper from Veda's Fudge Shop on the boardwalk. An announcement from an art gallery for a showing of Natalie Collins's photos.

Then I saw the photo.

Three women of different ages leaned against a decorative porch rail, smiling at the camera.

All at once I recognized the oldest of the three women. Lady Azura looked about twenty years younger than she was now; her hair was fuller and her lipstick much paler, but she still wore a long silk skirt and a flowy top. The woman next to her had dark hair in a ponytail. She wore a shirtdress and simple sandals. I suspected that this was Diana, my grandmother. Weird. She had the same intense gaze as Lady Azura.

A teenage girl in ripped jeans stood next to Diana.

I'd seen pictures of her before, although never that young. She looked exactly like me.

Natalie.

My mother.

Lady Azura's granddaughter.

Three generations of the family I'd never known I had.

And then I saw myself on that porch with them. I saw where I fit in.

I thought back to the day Dad and I moved in. I'd felt a powerful connection with Lady Azura. As time went on, I thought it had to do with our shared power. Now I knew it was something bigger.

We were family.

I peered closer at the three women.

They were my family.

Chapter 14

"Get a move on, Sara!" Dad called up to the third floor the next afternoon. "The Randazzos are expecting us. I can't wait to try my first feast of the seven fishes!"

I hadn't gone downstairs last night or this morning. I'd been hiding in my crafts room, working on a present for my great-grandmother.

Lady Azura.

I still couldn't believe it.

"I'm ready," I said, entering our family room. Dad was piling presents for Lily's brothers and sister into a large shopping bag. I added Lily's hat and the photo of Lily dancing that I'd printed out for her mom.

"You're wearing it?" He grinned when he noticed me.

"Do I look too pink?" I twirled, showing off the

outfit Janelle had bought for me at the mall.

"You look the right amount of pink," he said. "The sneakers balance it out."

I'd paired the outfit with my trusty old black Converse. It made me feel more me. I'd worn the clothes to make Dad happy. To show that I was always on his side. He'd sat with me late into the night, telling me funny stories about my mom.

"I need to tell you something," I said. "I've been keeping a secret from you."

"Really? Okay. Lay it on me."

"Dina doesn't like you. She doesn't want her mom to date you. She wanted me to convince you not to date her, either."

"Oh, is that it?" He chuckled. "I was expecting something much scarier than that."

"You know?"

He nodded. "I could tell. Dina's having a rough time. Her parents only got divorced recently. Dina thinks she can get them back together. She thinks I'm standing in their way."

"Are you?"

"I don't think so. Whether we're dating or not,

Janelle is not getting back with Dina's dad." He wrapped a scarf around his neck and grabbed his coat from the back of the chair. "Dina's unhappy right now. She's directing her unhappiness at me."

At me too, I thought.

"I feel bad for her." He handed me my coat.

"I'm not sure I do," I confessed, "but maybe now what she was trying to do makes some sort of sense. Even so, she's not nice."

"She'll warm up," Dad assured me as we headed downstairs.

"Doubtful." I had the feeling that now she'd be meaner than ever. Sad or not about the divorce, Dina didn't like her plans messed up. I'd messed them up big-time.

I froze on the last step. The French doors to the sitting room stood wide open. The tree glittered with silver tinsel and the bird ornaments. The birds looked magical, as if they had nested in a fairy-tale tree. Lady Azura perched stiffly on the edge of an armchair, her hands folded in her lap. She turned and caught my gaze.

My heart pounded, and for a moment, all I could

do was stare, as if I was meeting her for the first time.

She stood, shoulders back, chin high. Although she was shorter than I was, even in her black velvet heels, she appeared forceful and confident.

"So you know." It wasn't a question.

I walked toward her while Dad hung back. Was I supposed to hug her? Kiss her? Was that what you did with a great-grandmother?

"You were trying to tell me, sort of, in a round-about way for a while, weren't you?" I asked.

"I very much wanted you to know." Her voice was quiet but steady.

Then I realized that that was what the visions were leading me to as well. "Were you at my mom's funeral?" I asked suddenly. "Was it on a sunny day? Freshly cut grass all around?"

She wrinkled her brow. "Yes."

"You wore a black hat with a feather."

"Sara, how do you know—" Dad started to say.

Lady Azura cut Dad off. "I did." She didn't look surprised that I knew.

In my vision, I'd been watching her at my mother's funeral.

"What do you think of having me as a great-grand-mother?" Her eyes sought mine and held my gaze.

I handed her a square box.

She turned it about, inspecting my homemade wrapping paper. "What's this?"

"A Christmas present for you."

"You already gave me the best present," she said softly.

"It's another present, and the answer to the question you just asked."

She slit through the seams of the paper with her finger and meticulously unwrapped the box. I fiddled with the sleeves of my new shirt, pushing them up and down my arms. I hoped she understood what my present was trying to say.

She opened the box. Her posture stayed straight, and her grip remained steady. Only her face betrayed her. Tears streamed down her cheeks. Through puddles of black mascara, she stared at the ornament I'd made her.

I'd scanned the photo of her, Diana, and my mom into my computer and Photoshopped in a picture of me. I now stood next to my mother, who stood next to my grandmother, who stood next to my great-grandmother.

Four generations, all together.

I'd made a frame out of mini crystals and attached a silver ribbon to hang it on the tree.

"Our family is now complete." Lady Azura reached for my hand and squeezed it.

"Exactly." I grinned at her.

She hung the ornament in the middle of the tree. The three of us marveled at it, and Lady Azura never let go of my hand.

"Mike, be a dear, and unclasp my necklace before we go," Lady Azura asked. She held up the opal that rested on her ivory dress. "I don't need it anymore. All my wishes have come true."

While Dad helped Lady Azura remove her necklace, I wondered about the opal around my neck. The Dina wish hadn't worked out, but that was just a small wish. The big wish, the wish I hadn't said out loud but lived in my heart, was the one that had come true. I was starting to know my mother.

Lady Azura and I held hands all the way to Lily's house. Dad walked ahead to give us time together.

Cars lined the street. Family members crowded the Randazzos' front walk, their arms piled with present and foil-covered desserts.

"What should I call you now?" I asked Lady Azura.

"Great-grandmother sounds positively ancient! I couldn't bear it," she replied. "Let's stick with Lady Azura."

"Okay," I agreed. "But I'll probably think 'great-grandmother' in my head every time I say your name."

"And I'll probably know what you're thinking," she whispered. "Our secret."

As we headed toward the Randazzos' door, I suddenly remembered Lily's mom cautioning me to look and listen when I insisted that all my mom's family was dead. "Does Mrs. Randazzo know about you and me?" I asked.

"I believe Beth must know," she replied after a pause. "Beth's grandmother Lillian was my best friend. Ah, she was a wonderful, free soul. Reminds me so much of Lily. But Beth didn't know Natalie well. Your mother grew up in Neptune Beach, about twenty-five minutes from here. Beth met her a few times, and I believe she must have eventually put two and two together. You are the very image of your mother, Sara." Her grip on my hand tightened as she added, "And Beth knows me rather well, and you and I have a lot in common, wouldn't you agree?"

Mrs. Randazzo's behavior in the kitchen suddenly made a lot of sense. I wondered when she had figured it out.

"If you and I can both see spirits," I said, finally asking what I'd been wondering about, "does that mean it's a family thing?"

Lady Azura stopped on the walkway, letting others pass. "I used to think so. My mother could see them too. But then my Diana was born and she couldn't. Not at all. The power I had upset and confused her. It caused a lot of pain between us. Natalie couldn't either, so I thought the family line had run out." She smiled. "And then you arrived."

"Sara!" Lily squealed. She burst out of the door and wrapped me in a huge hug. "You won't believe what Aunt Angela got me for Christmas! Come see!"

I followed her through the crowded hall, leaving Lady Azura to talk with other guests. The house was filled with people talking, eating, and laughing. And then there were the other people. The spirits who had come for Christmas. They silently came and went, watching their loved ones, reaching out every now and then.

None of them bothered me. I could breathe easily, and I realized that, at least for today, Lady Azura was my White Light. I was happier than I'd ever been.

I couldn't wait to get to Lily's room and tell her that I got a great-grandmother for Christmas!

"Throw your coat on my bed," Lily said. There were already several coats piled on her purple comforter.

I pulled off my gloves and parka. As I was shoving the gloves in the pockets, my fingertips grazed something cold. I pulled out a necklace.

"What's that?" Lily moved to inspect the silver locket and chain in my hand.

"I don't know," I admitted. "I've never seen it before. It's not mine."

"But it was in your pocket," Lily said. "Did someone put it there?"

An angel was engraved on the face of the locket. Using my fingernails, I pried open its front. "Oh!" I cried.

"Who's that?" Lily asked, leaning over my shoulder.

My stomach had that fluttery feeling. "That's my mother."

"Really?" Lily reached for the locket, but I pulled away.

I couldn't let her touch it yet. A desire to keep it close overwhelmed me.

I fastened the clasp around my neck, and the locket slipped beneath my shirt. The cold metal touched my skin and instantly grew warm.

As I stood there, my mother's photo close to my heart, the locket radiated heat.

"I need to go see Lady Azura." My stomach was turning somersaults. I found her standing by my dad.

I lifted the locket from my sweater.

Dad's eyes went wide. He turned to Lady Azura. "Natalie gave you that? I thought it was lost."

Lady Azura nodded slightly. She seemed to be holding her breath.

Dad reached over and touched the angel. "I bought Natalie that locket when we first started dating." He smiled at me. "I'm glad you have it now, Sara. She would've wanted that."

"When did you—"

Lady Azura shot me a warning look that made me stop speaking.

"Mike, can you make me a plate?" She gestured toward a table piled high with cheese and grilled vegetables.

"You didn't put this in my pocket either, did you?" I asked Lady Azura once he left.

"No."

The warmth of the tiny locket spread over my body. A cozy, comforting warmth.

"It's a Christmas gift." She smiled at me. "You were visited."

My mom! I whirled around, looking for her.

"Can you see her?" I asked.

"No, but now you have proof she was here."

My hand reached for the locket. Maybe I couldn't see her now, but I had the feeling that someday I would.

Want to know what happens to Sara next?

Here's a sneak peek at the next book in the series:

Moment
of
Truth

A gust of icy wind blew off the ocean and swirled down the back of my neck. I zipped my parka all the way up and pulled my hat all the way down, over my ears.

This was my first East Coast winter. Freezing-cold weather was new to me. I shivered and hugged my arms tightly. Then I scanned the boardwalk, searching for Lily.

Lily Randazzo was many things: a lively, bubbly, warm person; my first-ever best friend; a member of a big, bustling family that had welcomed me, an only child, with open arms.

But here's one thing Lily was not: punctual.

I leaned against the doorway of Scoops Ice Cream Parlor and closed my eyes. Thank goodness it was Friday afternoon. I'd had a lot of trouble concentrating in school all week. I was ready for the weekend.

For the past several nights, a spirit had been keeping me awake. It was the spirit of a sobbing, long-dead woman, who shared the old house I lived in with my father and great-grandmother.

Just one of the spirits, that is.

I've seen spirits since I was a little kid. But last summer, when we moved to Stellamar, I'd started seeing a lot more. My great-grandmother, Lady Azura, can see them too. The sobbing woman spirit lived in a room on the second floor of our house. She's been there since we moved in, but her weeping and wailing had grown louder and more insistent in recent weeks. I couldn't get much sleep some nights because of it. This week, it had been most nights.

My phone buzzed. A text from Lily.

SORRY! RUNNING BEHIND, WHAT ELSE IS NEW :)

I texted her back. My fingers were numb from taking pictures without gloves on, so I kept it short.

CU SOON.

I pulled out my camera to snap some pictures. A jogger passed me. She was running with a large, friendly-looking dog on a leash. *Snap-snap-snap.* I took a series of motion shots of them as they passed me. The light was perfect—late afternoon on a late February day, the shadows rapidly lengthening, the sun dipping low in the sky over the ocean horizon.

Snap-snap-snap. Until recently, I used to only take pictures of objects. Never people. But lately that had changed. I'd joined the school newspaper as a photographer, and most news stories involved people. I had gotten pretty comfortable shooting pictures of people. One more thing that was different about me now.

So much had changed in the past few months.

I scanned the distant boardwalk.

Who was *that*?

I lowered my camera and peered at the person making his way toward me along the boardwalk.

He was still far in the distance. He wasn't wearing a coat. Oddly, he did not seem to mind the cold.

I raised my camera. Zoomed in. Snapped a bunch of pictures of him. As he got a little closer, I could see that he was about my age—maybe twelve or thirteen—and that he was very cute, and tall, with shaggy dark hair.

Then a shock rippled though me. I lowered my camera again and stared at the boy.

He was a spirit.

What gave him away to me was the light. All around him, a light shimmered, and the air sort of rippled as he walked. I snapped another picture. He still didn't seem to have noticed me, so I took a few more.

I hadn't seen that many spirits my age. Most were old, or at least a lot older than me. I'd have to tell Lady Azura about this. Lately I'd been telling her about all the spirits I saw. It felt good to tell someone. For a change.

Lady Azura was a professional fortune-teller. She had been communicating with spirits for decades. It was all still pretty new to me. She was helping me to understand my powers. That was one of the main reasons we moved to Stellamar. But my dad hadn't told me she was my great-grandmother until recently. Just this past Christmas.

The spirit moved closer. He was maybe twenty feet away. I definitely had to stop taking pictures of him now.

"Boo!"

I whirled around.

It was Lily, of course.

"I so got you that time!" she said. Next to her were Marlee and Avery, both smiling and shaking their heads as if to say they took no responsibility for what Lily did.

"Yep, you got me," I said, happy to see my friends.

Forgetting all about spirit boy.

"Why are you standing outside? It's, like, seventy-five below zero out here, and you're from California!" Lily exclaimed.

"I was just taking some pictures," I said. "The light is so pretty right now."

"Light, schmight. You artists." She held open the door of Scoops and corralled the three of us ahead of her.

"Lily!" yelled the teenage girl behind the counter. It was Dawn Marie, Lily's cousin. Scoops was owned by Lily's "uncle," Paul—not a real uncle, but a close family friend. The fact that he wasn't an actual blood relation of Lily's was unusual. Most of the time, you couldn't throw a rock in Stellamar, New Jersey, without hitting someone who was related to Lily Randazzo.

"What'll it be?" asked Dawn Marie.

"The usual?" Lily asked, turning toward Marlee, Avery, and me. We all nodded. We usually get the "original" sundae, which comes with two scoops— Dawn Marie gave you extra-big scoops, too.

We made our way to our favorite table.

"So are you pumped for the morp?" Avery asked.

I looked at her blankly. "The what?"

Avery giggled. "I forget how new you still are! It's the big middle school semiformal. Girls are supposed to ask guys. Morp is 'prom' spelled backward. So it's like a winter prom for the middle school, but with a cool twist."

I looked at her in horror. Nothing about asking a boy to go to a dance with you sounded cool to me.

"You don't *have* to go as a couple," Lily explained. "But if you do, it just means you have to invite the guy. So are you going to ask Jayden?"

I sat back in my chair. The idea of asking a boy to a dance filled me with dread. Even if the boy was Jayden, who I was pretty comfortable with these days.

"Are you going to ask Jack?" Avery asked Lily.

"I'm not sure," said Lily. "Jack is definitely at the top of my list. I'm—" She stopped midsentence.

"Don't. Look. Now," Lily whispered, leaning in toward the three of us. "But the cutest boy I have ever laid eyes on just walked in."

I swiveled in my chair.

It was the boy from the boardwalk. The spirit. I whipped around to look back at my friends. They could see him, too! *How was that possible?*